I0603309

Summer in the City

Reed Lavender: 3

Ashley Capes

Summer in the City
(Reed Lavender: 3)
Copyright © 2021 by Ashley Capes

Cover: Illustration by Vivid Covers
Layout & Typeset: Close-Up Books

ISBN-978-0-6487705-4-1

www.ashleycapes.com

Published by Close-Up Books
Melbourne, Australia

For Brooke

Chapter 1.

The Radiant King had not attacked, seemingly content to let them approach the city, unobstructed by any more servants.

And so far, Reed had not been able to broach the subject of Emma staying 'out of it' as Lina suggested. *Don't know how I feel about the idea either.*

Instead, he frowned over the steering wheel as the engine hummed along the black highway. All around, the green fields were turning into empty developments with gentle roads and streetlights void of globe or light. Further ahead, walls and steel columns rose up, wavering beneath the glare of heat haze.

But the sun above did not seem so strong.

Not that the word 'above' really means much in this place.

More important questions had to be dealt with. *Like, what will we find in the city?* The Radiant King was hardly defeated, despite the death of the shell. *And Enki still has to pay for using Dad's body.*

"I don't think we're getting closer, you know," Max said from the back seat.

Reed glanced in the mirror. His cousin was swirling a finger behind Emma's head, and a single strand of her hair followed his movements. Behind him in turn, sitting in the tray with all their supplies – including water from Dionysus' fountain – Diego and Lina spoke to one another.

"Maybe." Reed tapped his fingers on the wheel. It had been a little while already. "What do we do about it?"

"No idea."

"Well, thank the gods you've come along, then," he replied, his tone snappy.

"Steady there, old stick. We'll figure it out."

Emma glanced at him. "Are you all right, Reed?"

"Maybe." Apparently he had plenty of left-over anger and frustration, and all of it directed at the Radiant King. Well, most of it. *Have to save some for that prick Dunstall.* But Elise would have to wait a little longer still... a promise he grew weary of making. *And immediately breaking.*

That would change soon enough.

First, the city.

She raised an eyebrow. "Maybe, huh?"

"Just thinking."

"About your father?"

"And Elise, and what's ahead. And how we're going to get out of this shit-hole, once we know what's going on."

"Leave that to me," Max replied. "I think I can get us out via the Fringe if need be; Mother left me a little something for that."

"And reaching the city?" Emma asked.

Max stared ahead for a moment longer, rubbing his

temples. "Ah, got it." He clapped his hands together. "Just turn around and then start reversing, head for the city that way."

"Really?"

"Let's try it; I think that's the trick."

Reed shrugged as he slowed, then performed a fairly smooth U-turn, before doing as instructed. He kept a straight line but didn't drive too fast. The passage of air against his forearm and face had changed, and a scent of vine-tomatoes had joined it.

More of Feronia's influence? Yet he saw no gardens.

"What are you doing?" Lina called from the tray.

"Trying something," Max replied.

Reed straightened in his seat. Between glances in the rear-view mirror and the back windscreen, he saw two shimmering cities.

Only, the one beyond the windscreen was looming larger, even as he eased his foot from the pedal. The walls revealed themselves to be tightly-packed buildings of stone and steel, all with banks of darkened windows, like apartment building blocks lacking even a hint of reflective glass.

"How did that...?"

Farther within, skyscrapers towered above, some shaped vaguely like driven swords or spears – and these *did* catch the light, flashing as if set between massive beams. But the sky was clear and blue overhead.

The road came to a halt in some sort of terminal... an empty taxi rank, complete with yellow and silver shelters and painted numbers for bays. Reed pulled into one and cut the engine.

Twin pedestrian lanes ran through a blooming garden.

At a glance, it was immaculately maintained, with hedge boxes of blue and white flowers, rounded plots for elms and a lawn so consistently green, it might as well have been coloured with a paint bucket. Bench seats and picnic tables were empty, along with the footpaths, where open shops gleamed electric. There was even the scent of fried chicken from somewhere!

"This is better than the towns, so far," Lina said as she appeared beside Reed, standing outside the car. She pulled open his door. "Look, he's remembered to put in those bins with cigarette trays."

"And what is the name of the city council there?" Max asked, pointing.

"Ah..."

The description of 'City Council Waste Management' was clear in English, but the name of that council was in no recognisable language. Reed glanced to Emma, who was frowning at it. "I think this is a language of the Splinter Gods."

"So it seems," Max agreed.

Diego folded his arms where he stood in his hulking minotaur form, golden horns gleaming from a dark mane. "I do not recall Enki listed among them."

"Neither do I..." Emma trailed off, then pointed. "Look."

At the end of the block, a man in a dark blue suit was crossing the street, briefcase in hand. He wore a wide-brimmed hat that could have been an Akubra, and seemed to be whistling.

"Let's see what he has to say," Reed said.

Chapter 2.

But the fellow and his blue suit seemed to be in quite the hurry – already a block away when they turned into the street, and nor did he stop when Reed called out. It left the mostly empty shopfronts and the still-present scent of roasting chicken from up ahead.

"He was real, right?" Reed asked as he leant against a streetlamp a moment.

"Indeed," Max said. He stared after the fellow, though his eyes were not focused on anything in particular. "In fact, there are nineteen other people here – they all have life spans too – but no true sense of Enki."

"Isn't there something unusual about them though?" Lina asked. "It's like I'm being blocked... I can't get a clear view of what exactly is strange."

"Sounds like Enki's work," he replied.

"Should I go back to collect one of the barrels?" Diego asked.

Reed spread his hands. "I imagine we'll have to drive around sooner or later – it's a big city. Maybe it depends on how deep we go now? Or maybe we should anyway, Enki might be in retreat, but he could have other servants."

"Let's just visit the chicken place," Lina suggested. "It's right around the corner, and whoever's working probably won't ignore us like Mr Briefcase."

"Why not?" Max said. "We've already strolled in this far and I could almost convince myself to eat some more human grub."

"No-one really says that, Max," Emma said with a smile.

"Really? That's disappointing, I've always like it."

"Let's make a move then," Reed said as he started forward.

He led them past several souvenir shops in a row, windows crammed with opal-themed everything; cushions, hats, bracelets and even fluffy koala bears with opal eyes – the animals appearing somehow zombie-like. And the goods really had been stuffed in there too, beside books and DVDs, featuring pearlescent rainbows fighting for space. *Like a more unhinged Swanston Street.* Most items were pressed up against the glass too, as though the shopkeeper had simply continued shoving items into the display.

Other shops were empty, the electrical wires hanging from half-finished ceilings and even featuring empty packs of cigarettes and bottle caps in dusty corners.

Lina directed him to turn at an intersection, traffic lights dark, where they came face to face with a bronze statue upon a podium. A sporting figure... *sort of.* Though the athlete was a specimen of perfect proportions, the man wore studded boots, volleyball shorts and shoulder pads, and the oddity was topped off by a swimming cap. In one hand, he held a twisted mix between a hockey stick and a tennis racquet.

The other hand was raised in a triumphant fist, and every detail had been sculpted with great care.

"Admiring old Fox Robington, eh?"

Reed turned.

A woman stood in the doorway of the chicken take-away joint, the nearby sparkling glass revealing a golden array of meat. She wore a pleasant smile, her cheeks rosing as she waved them over. "Come in, you all look hungry, am I right?"

"A little," Reed said, but he didn't move at first. "It seems a bit quiet today, doesn't it?"

She shrugged. "Been like this since I was a kid. You'd have to go back to the glory days of Robington to see this place busy, but we get by."

Reed opened his mouth to ask exactly who she meant by 'we' but Max spoke first.

"Robington is an interesting name, isn't it?" He said as he waved everyone after, allowing the woman to seat them inside a spacious place set with red chairs and white tables, sparkling tinsel Christmas decorations hanging from the ceiling.

"Some might say," she said with a chuckle. "You might be able to ask him about it yourself, if you're lucky."

"He drops in sometimes?"

The owner sighed. "Well, not so often lately. I understand he's in recovery. Old injury flaring up, you see. In any case, let me welcome you to Raelene's. How about I get you some menus?"

"Ah, perhaps just a drink?" Reed asked.

Max held up a finger. "Now now, cousin, you should

at least order something for yourself, and Emma. You skipped lunch, remember?" His smile was friendly but his gaze seemed more insistent.

"How about a couple of chicken burgers then?" he asked Raelene. He glanced at Emma, who did not object.

"Coming right up." The woman headed behind the glass counter with its neat register, then into the back where she spoke to someone. The hiss of meat striking something hot followed.

"Why are you suddenly so desperate to feed us?" Reed asked.

"Just trying to learn a little something," Max replied. "For one, why hasn't the delightful Raelene reacted to Diego?"

Reed glanced at the minotaur, then hung his head a moment. *Idiot. So focused on having her* talk *that you forgot what was right in front of you.* Another of his rules – reactions were worth a thousand words. "Right."

Lina nodded. "We can also take this chance to ask her about other visitors."

"And if we stay here, we might meet one of her other customers without having to go looking for them," Emma added. "We're also still reasonably close to the ute, this way."

"So I see," Reed said, raising his hands as he slouched into the hard plastic of his chair. "Looks like you're all paying better attention that I am."

"Something on your mind?" Max asked.

"Plenty... but let's save it for later," he said, straightening a little. "Looks like Emma was on the money."

A tall figure approached the shop's door, dressed in a

long overcoat of yellow, tanned skin and dark curls spilling across her shoulders. Her face seemed a little too angular, though she was certainly human.

She paused upon seeing them, eyes widening. "Wow! It's certainly been a while since we've seen visitors in Parginos, welcome to you all."

"Thank you," Reed replied. "It's a fascinating city." He waited a moment but the woman didn't respond to Diego, either. Instead, she asked to join them.

Diego stood and pulled a chair free from a nearby table, moving it to their own. "Please do."

"Thank you," she replied as she sat with a grin. "I'm Kiri and I'm the Watch here."

"The Watch?" Max asked.

"It's like a mix between police and military. Ideally, there'd be more than just me but it's not like when I was younger," she explained, though did not offer any more. Still, the phrase about her youth was not unlike what Raelene had claimed.

Lina smiled at the woman. "Have you lived here a long time?"

"All my life."

"And it's a nice place?"

Kiri pursed her lips. "Almost always... but, every now and then one of us goes back to the First Day and right before, sometimes it's dangerous."

"The First Day?"

"Oh, that's right, you probably haven't heard of it. I don't think the other visitors had anything like it, either. You must be from pretty far away?"

"We are," Lina said. "Is there a First Day coming soon?

Are we in danger, if it is?"

"Oh, no." Kiri shook her head, curls bouncing. "No tourists have ever been hurt, so you don't have to worry. Mind if I place an order before we talk more? I'd love to hear more about where you're from."

"We'd love to chat, of course," Lina replied.

Kiri set off for the counter with a smile and Reed leant across the table, lowering his voice. "Let's find out about this First Day."

"And what happened to the other visitors," Emma added.

The others were already nodding. Reed glanced back to Kiri where the unusual woman waited at the counter, her coat revealing no hint of weapons that he could see. A little shiver ran across his shoulders, despite the warmth of the shop and the two people they'd met so far.

Because just like the rest of the Radiant King's domain, the city of Parginos was not quite as it should be – and the oddities far outweighed whatever refinements Enki had made this time around.

So what's the purpose of this place, then?

Chapter 3.

Raelene's voice echoed from the kitchen. "That you, Kiri?"

"Sure is."

"Won't be long – the usual okay?"

"Yes, please," Kiri said, then returned to her chair. As she settled, a strange sound echoed softly in the room. Reed frowned as he tried to figure it out. There was a rhythm, choppy but not made by an instrument he recognised. Something that could have been a guitar chimed fluttering notes, the tempo double time to the 'beat'. There was even a voice, but the words were simply promises. Literal promises, as a woman listed things she could guarantee – from furniture to undying love.

Her voice seemed familiar... *It's supposed to be a song?*

Lina and Max were already explaining Melbourne to Kiri – and getting most of it right too, when Reed stood to cross the floor. He stopped near a speaker, eyes widening as he looked up at the steely mesh.

The voice was familiar because... because he recognised it?

From a long time ago.

"Mum?"

Reed clenched a fist. It *was* her! There was something about the soothing tone, the memory like a slap. Reed spun. "Kiri, who am I hearing right now?"

The young woman turned, a little taken aback, but she still smiled. "You like it, huh? It's by Capri, she's the Singer. I love her voice."

He hurried back to his seat, trying not to run. "She lives here in the city?"

"Well, I don't know. You can't meet her; she's just always been the one to make the Songs."

"Are you sure?"

"Ah, maybe old Robington would know."

Then that's who we need to speak to next. "Do you know how to reach him?"

"Here you go," Raelene said as she approached the table, and set down two plates. Two large chicken burgers with cheese and aioli, nestled within a ring of large-cut chips. It looked and smelled quite good.

"Eat up, Reed," Max said. "And give Kiri a break, will you? She's probably got better things to do than answer your silly questions."

"Oh, it's no trouble."

Reed shook his head even as he picked up his fork and took a bite of a chip – crispy and salty. *Perfect. But Max is right, no good scaring off the locals. Breathe.* "No, he's right. It can wait."

Dad's words rang in his mind. *If you can find your mother, the two of you might just be able to get me out of here.*

"You were going to tell us a little about the First Day," Lina was saying.

"Right. Well, it's hard to explain. When it's near, you visit the Fountain of Leaves. That's where the ritual happens. You don't remember much afterwards, but you get a chance to do a better job or sometimes a different one."

Well, there's a lot going on there. But Reed let Lina continue.

"Wow, that sounds pretty different to what we have. Can visitors see the ritual?"

Kiri shook her head. "It's always private."

"But when you get there, do you just automatically know what to do?" Max asked.

"Oh sorry, no. Feronia helps us." A muted sound, like a phone vibrating, buzzed from her coat. She pulled out a sleek mobile and answered with a frown. "Is something wrong?"

A muffled voice answered, a man, perhaps.

"I'll head over there now," she said, then hung up before standing. "Sorry to leave so suddenly, but I have to check up on someone."

"Trouble?" Max asked.

"Nothing I haven't dealt with before," she replied, her expression becoming firmer as she strode to the counter and then called to Raelene, promising to return for lunch.

"Should we follow her?" Emma asked once the door swung closed behind Kiri and her striking yellow coat.

"Tempting," Lina replied. "I can almost feel the disturbance... but this might be a better time to find the so-called Fountain of Leaves. I'm curious about this First Day thing."

"True." Reed took a big bite of his burger as he nodded. *Damn it, I am hungry after all.* "But let's bring Dionysus' water along."

***

Reed again found himself gripping the wheel a little hard. *Is it just like Dad claimed? Mum is here somewhere.*

The streets were wide and clear of obstruction, tidy too. Tall office blocks and apartment buildings of painted brick were wedged between take-away shops and restaurants, gleaming clean, their bar stools empty, tablecloths untouched.

He also passed a closed off street, the maintenance equipment just a little 'off' since the witches hats were closer to yellow than orange. Which didn't look right at all, but the traffic cones were not so unusual compared to three music stores lined up beside each other in a single block.

Reed parked before the only open shop, a giant record hanging in the front window. The label was black and white, geometric pattern, but offered no name of artist nor the store itself.

Emma frowned across at him. "Reed?"

"I just want to check something," he said as he hopped out, boots grinding faint gravel from a recently repaired pothole. *Not that we've seen another vehicle yet.* "This seems like a good place."

"For what?" she called from the car.

"Reed, what are you up to?" Max added. "We're not on a shopping spree."

"I won't be long," Reed replied as he pushed the door open to the jingle of a bell.

Inside, skylights lit walls and racks lined with LPs, CDs, cassette tapes and even 8-tracks too – the range of artwork just as varied as in a real store... but something was amiss.

One cover caught his eye.

A demon carried a bundle of sticks upon its back, but wore a look of shock, as a shadowy figure seemed to have hurled a golden tuba at the creature. "What is this...?" He lifted the LP free, and upon the back waited a list of songs and performers... Robert Plant, Yo-Yo Ma, Keith Jarrett and Dimebag Darrell. "No drummer," he said, a little bemused. *By all the gods, what would that sound like?*

The door bell rang again – Emma entered, looking around with a slight frown.

"Welcome to *Good Vertebrae's*!" a cheery voice announced.

A young man wearing a leather jacket and a 50s-style circle skirt stood by the counter, which had been empty a moment ago. Beads stirred in the doorway behind him, which no doubt led to the back room.

"Thank you," Emma replied, hesitating for just a moment.

"Can I help you at all?"

Despite the odd attempt at a Beach Boys pun, the store did have one thing going for it – the music wasn't deafening; it was actually possible to have a conversation. And the music that *did* play was the same... 'non-music' from Raelene's, where dissonant sounds with vague melodies supported a woman reciting more promises. *That is* definitely *Mum's voice.*

Reed nodded. "I hope so."

Chapter 4.

The young man walked over, revealing green eyes to go with his smile – the colour almost supernaturally bright, up close. "I'll do my best."

"I'm after some information about the singer that's playing right now."

"Oh, you don't have her songs at home? Sorry, I thought Capri was everywhere." He offered a grin, shuffling his feet. "It's not long after my First Day, takes a while to remember everything, you know?"

Not really. "No problem," Reed said. "So, she's only here in Parginos?"

"I think so, I mean, I haven't seen her myself so I'm not sure."

"Oh?"

"Yeah, she's supposedly in the Garden but I've never been there either."

"What about posters or a CD, could we see one of those?" Emma asked, and it seemed she'd picked up on the fact that he was chasing clues, but he'd have to tell her why.

The lad winced. "Gee, I hate to let you both down but I can't do that either. Let me show you what I mean."

He led them to the counter, which was covered in stacks of CDs rising from packing foam, then through the bead-curtain into the back room. There, a small table and chair stood surrounded by unopened boxes. *A lot of stock for a city with twenty people.* But it was not that fact, nor the bagged lunch, that caught his eye – it was the polished Gramophone with its digital display.

Fourteen thousand songs and currently playing number seven hundred and two. The song was exactly three minutes long. Reed rushed through the math in his head – a twenty-nine-day cycle would pass before anyone heard the same song again, providing all songs were about the same length. *That is... unusual.*

"We don't sell Capri's music, you see. Everyone gets it at home or work, for free via their Gramophone."

Not quite that unusual, considering radios and so-called 'smart speakers'. "So, does she ever play any live gigs?"

The shopkeeper frowned. "Gigs?"

"Like a live concert, in person."

"Oh, I understand now. Maybe in the Garden?" He took a breath and sudden tears appeared in his bright eyes. "But I don't really know. Sorry again,"

Reed raised his hands. "Oh, it's fine. Thanks for the help. Maybe I could buy something else?"

"Sure, that'd be great. Just take your pick and it's yours."

"We don't need to pay?" Emma asked.

"No, it's cool."

Just like in the cafe... no money required. And they all seem cheerful and friendly, even melodramatic. "Then, we can just choose something on the way out?"

"Yeah, that's how it works. Sorry again, I keep forgetting."

"Thanks, that sounds great," Reed said as he returned to the shop floor. He retrieved the LP featuring its odd mix of musicians, the one he'd first noticed, and its tuba-attack artwork. "How about this?"

The young man pumped his fist. "Oh yeah! Great choice, that's the last album from the *Hindenburg Silks* – you'll love it!"

Reed had to smile; the enthusiasm was not so far removed from a normal retail assistant in a normal music store in that sense. "Well, thanks again," he said on his way out.

"Come back on your way home, if you can."

Outside, Reed and Emma exchanged a glance. "I'm having trouble keeping up with this place," she said.

"I know what you mean."

She didn't head for the ute right away. "So, hold on a minute. What was this trip for?"

"Well, to me, Capri sounds like my mother."

"What? Really?"

He nodded.

"Oh... Reed, then let's find out somehow."

"Thanks. My only idea is to smash my way into that Garden and see if she's really here," he replied. "But I think we need to check out the Fountain of Leaves first. Maybe it's the same place."

"Could be."

"No gift-wrapping?" Max called from the back seat.

"All right, we're coming." Reed hopped back into the driver's seat then frowned at his cousin. "I was following a lead. Supposedly Capri can be found in the garden, the singer we heard in the cafe."

"Meaning?"

"Meaning, I think it's Mum – I recognise the voice."

Max took a deep breath. "Well. You did say that your father alluded to finding her here."

"But you don't sense anything that could be her?"

"No, sorry to say."

"Me either." Reed fired the engine and pulled back into the street, easing his way past the empty shops for now. "We should probably find the Fountain of Leaves first, anyway. Can you sense that?"

"Very much so. Just follow my directions."

"Perfect."

Ahead, a figure upon a bicycle approached from an empty fast-food parking lot, keeping close to the footpath. When they drew near enough, Reed squinted. The rider seemed to be part cat, part human, still dressed in human clothes... *Like the* Wind in the Willows*?*

The bike even featured a wicker basket full of silvery fish.

The rider waved cheerfully, then checked on their haul before turning down a narrow side-street. *This place continues to baffle, but at least it's consistent.* The cat was probably not something to chase down for now; if nothing else, it did seem to explain why Raelene and Kiri hadn't batted an eyelid when it came to Diego.

"Interesting," Max said, staring after it. "Oh, left at that green post box by the way."

Reed turned the wheel, the new street just as spacious and empty, but now lined with the glass-covered, angular-design of schools, along with outdoor pools and parks. Most of the greenery was made up of spiky natives, banksias blooming a pinkish red, but there was a massive Dragon Blood Tree too. Its branches spread up and out, almost like pale stone beneath the green foliage.

"That's a tree from the around the Arabian Sea," Emma said, frowning up at it as they circled the low stone walls of the park.

"Is the climate here so different?" Max asked.

Reed glanced at his cousin, who was grinning from where he now lay stretched across the back seat.

"Two more lefts and we'll reach the gate," his cousin added.

"Right."

Reed made the turns, then slowed the ute to bump up the small slope leading to the garden. Not far in, the road became blocked by huge wrought-iron gates, in turn flanked by twin elms. The gates stood two storeys tall, and bore spiked decorations at the top, though the vertical bars within had been arranged to appear as open roses, leaves and thorns just as detailed.

Beautiful work, but accented by an interesting choice.

Clean white skulls hung from the gate, from human to bird and smaller mammals, perhaps dogs and cats too... and each one bearing a flower wreath, the fresh blooms in pink, red, blue and white.

Lina appeared by the driver's window, staring into the greenery beyond. "Everyone be wary; the fountain is definitely outside our realm."

Unusual for a place that sounded as though it was related to Death. "What can you sense?" Reed asked.

"Order, but a cycle of diminishing returns... one they

either don't realise, or care about."

"Are you talking about some sort of evolution?" Emma asked.

"That's as good a word as any."

Reed cut the engine. "Are we actually prepared?"

"We are," she said. "But you know what they say about surprises."

Max appeared beside her. "Enki is still reeling; I feel nothing like our Radiant King here precisely. Feronia is not fully present, either... but if there's something I don't like the look of, we're skipping out via the Fringe."

"You're sure that'll work?" Reed asked.

"Trust me, Reed. I'm watching every single thing in this city *very* closely."

Chapter 5.

Like the others, 'holy' water from Dionysus' fountain dripped from Reed's hair and clothes, even his fingertips, as he led them up the path and toward the Fountain.

Leaves fell from the elm and beech, green and faintly golden where they spread across the smooth path. Birds chirped too, an entirely tranquil scene topped off by the welcome scent of flowers; a sweet walk through an ordered park... but the looming branches of the Dragon Blood Tree cast a long shadow across the Fountain.

Reed slowed.

Not that different to the gates, really. The Fountain of Leaves was a house-sized mound of pale skulls – rising up to support huge, twin rib bones of *something.* The ribs met their points, creating the outline not dissimilar to a pear.

Water did not spray forth from the fountain; instead, it ran down the structure in a thin film, like a liquid skin, glittering despite the shade. Here, perfume from the flowerbeds was overwhelmed by the sting of hot sand, though not a single grain was visible.

When Reed stopped before the base, the glittering revealed itself – in part – as golden runes painted upon each bone; these too just as varied as those upon the gates. But like the language upon the bins near the entry, the words were empty of meaning. And the glimmer itself still didn't make sense, given the shade.

"What now?" Reed asked. "I feel like... it's not that different from the 'water wheel' in the greenhouse."

"There are similarities, but it's more like a garden bed," Max said as he took another step closer. "All the people within the city, they have anchors here, like seeds. They're growing on a cycle, but bound."

"Why?" Emma asked.

"Indeed."

Diego set their depleted water jug down a moment, resting his axe upon a shoulder. "Hard to know what our next step should be, isn't it? This doesn't strike me as something we can break, but I fear we must, even without knowing its purpose."

"One thing is clear," Lina said as she skipped up and into the air, as though climbing invisible steps, where she began to examine the ribs. "Neither Feronia nor Enki are 'here' precisely."

"What does that mean, Lina?" Reed asked.

"You've wounded Enki more than we assumed. It could be weeks before he makes his next move, whatever that may be. And somehow, Feronia is linked to him."

"She's the one maintaining the city," Max added.

"Then we strike now, while they're weakened, yes?" Diego said, hefting his blade.

"It's probably our best chance but the fallout could be

significant," Max said. "Can you feel it?"

The minotaur paused, then lowered his weapon. "Ah."

"The Fountain is linked to the city, somehow," Lina explained as she hopped down. "If I bothered to compare, I'd say that this place is about the same size as Melbourne."

"So, does that mean there's some risk Melbourne too?" Emma asked.

"Yes."

Max raised a finger. "Force isn't our only option, if we just figure a few more things out and think it through."

Reed nodded as he began to pace, though confidence wasn't high. Hard to come up with something on the spot, when it came to dealing with an ancient Sumerian God and a reborn but presumably still mostly-broken part of a Roman Goddess. *But why did they build such a city in the first place? And all the other towns and buildings... like, 'tests' for this place.*

Hissing from the fountain.

Reed spun. The symbols were changing, darkening from gold to orange and then red as steam rose. Shadows lengthened swiftly, spreading from no particular source. Bird-song faded.

"Everyone to me," Max cried.

Reed turned for Emma, but she was already pulling him close to Max and Lina. Diego had leapt beside the two already, barrel under one arm, and then a grey film snapped down around the park.

Searing air hit Reed's skin, stinging his eyeballs and somehow filling his ears too. He clenched his jaw but the oppressive heat had not finished – it drove him to his knees where he gasped for oxygen.

The world flickered in flashes of colour – colour that stung like ice compared to the Fringe, and then it was back to the heat again. Max was shouting but the words were not clear. Why wasn't the water or their protective markings making a difference? He twisted to face Emma, who was curled into a ball.

Lina bent by him, then turned to Max. "Hurry!"

And then sweet, cool darkness.

"Sorry, you can open your eyes now, you two," Max was saying.

Reed found his face mere centimetres from carpet, a dark, faded blue with a musty scent. Sweat dripped from his forehead and the carpet drank of it greedily. He rolled onto his back with another gasp, just lying back to breathe a moment. Emma seemed to be doing the same.

"Max, she's not doing too well." Lina did not sound confident.

Reed sat up swiftly.

Lina knelt beside Emma, one pale hand upon her brow and the other holding her glasses. Emma was still breathing but they were shallow gasps now.

"Take her to Apollo. Or Asclepius if he's busy, and I'll follow," Max said. *He* didn't sound as concerned, but then, 'flippant' might well be carved upon his tombstone one day.

Reed took Emma's hand. "Wait, what's happening?"

Max sighed. "I misjudged, but Lina will get her healed."

"Don't worry, Reed." Lina slid her arms beneath Emma and rose smoothly before blinking out of sight.

"Here." Max helped Reed up and into his chair, where he slumped despite the tension within his limbs. The sweat soaked through his clothes and into the fabric. *Was it just the stress of the Fringe that hit her so hard?* "I'll get you some water, then you should rest."

"Once I know she's safe," Reed replied.

Max snapped his fingers and a tall glass of water appeared in his hand. "Drink up."

Reed lifted the glass, cold, soothing liquid breaking over his lips and tongue, cascading down his throat like the purist of blessings. All the clichés about gold and desserts came rushing to the fore. *All apt, each and every bloody one of them.* He put the empty glass down on the coffee table. "What happened back there?"

"Emma simply wasn't prepared – I tried to shield her but it wasn't quite enough. She'll recover in no time; she's tough, even for a human."

"Max, that had better be true."

"It is."

Again, no hesitation from the man. *A good sign, surely.* "All right. What about the Fountain, then?"

"That's a little more complex. Lina wasn't wrong about Enki and Feronia being out of action for a time, but that... thing was going to draw us in, all of us. We'd be part of the cycle then."

"You and Lina too? And Diego?" Reed blinked. "Where's Diego?"

"Reporting to Mars. And yes, it could have absorbed us too – there are more than a few things that aren't gods which could cause us trouble."

"But?"

"With this fountain thing... since I don't really know what it is, I didn't want to risk it. Maybe I could break out easily enough, maybe not. The thing is new amongst the universe, even if it does seem linked to Feronia."

"Too new?"

He grinned. "Troubling, isn't it?"

"Yes."

"Well, I'll do some more poking around, so why don't you rest for a while. I estimate we've got a couple of weeks or so before Enki is ready to take another shell, or maybe something worse, so we just need to strike before then."

"Right, but what about–"

His cousin was already gone.

Chapter 6.

Reed woke to a quiet darkness, open blinds letting pale moonlight paint itself across his walls, the couch and the television cabinet alike.

"Huh." He wasn't shivering, the way a winter night should have left him, especially after sleeping in a chair, with no blanket and no heater for comfort. *A nice surprise, I guess.* Reed shrugged his way out of the chair with a sigh.

In the kitchen, he fumbled for his phone where it lay on the table, frowning at the blank screen. *Flat, of course. Emma should be back by now.* Once it was plugged in, he tapped at the phone until the screen blinked on.

Both date and time were wrong: November thirteenth.

He gave the phone a shake, a useless gesture, then restarted it again.

When his mobile returned to life, it was still glitching to November. "Whatever." Reed dialled Emma's phone; message bank only, and left a message before pacing the kitchen, clomping across the tiles.

She's probably fine. Lina would have got her to Apollo,

got her all fixed up, and she was probably just asleep, recovering.

Reed paused at the sink. *A couple of weeks before the Radiant King can strike again, huh?* "I hope you're right, Max."

His cousin probably wasn't mistaken.

When meant it was time to book a flight.

And break some rules... it was past time to finally live up to his word. The first problem was deciding precisely who to call. Who, if anyone, would be willing to help out?

All children of the gods were off the table, considering the threats from Aunty... but there was no other way. Tracking down Dunstall could take weeks, especially if he was still overseas. No chance of getting help from Duong either, and it wouldn't do to put the guy in any more danger.

Especially with my doll still happily mute in solitary.

But it had to be someone – or some*thing* – that he could exercise some degree of control over, while also being able to pay the debt.

"Just what you need, dickhead. Another debt," Reed muttered as he strode down the hall to the 'spare' room, which was a generous term, considering that he had to shift stacked boxes, an exercise bike, an antique stereo and two old, faded armchairs just to reach the wardrobe.

But once he slid the doors open, he reached into his shelf for what his father had jokingly called the 'Little Book of Summoning'. Black cover, silver text – quite a nicely produced item, despite the yellowed pages within.

An Imp will be enough, surely?

He hauled the book free, then let it thud against one of the armchairs, dust puffing up from the seat as he flipped through the pages. The bold strokes of the Latin and detailed, sometimes grotesque pictures spoke to the gravity of the contents, but he did not linger on his way to the section on lesser demons.

"Here we go." The recipe was simple enough; blood for the contract and a bit of chalk for the symbology, but he didn't have a whole lot of ash on hand. *It's not like every building has a fireplace here in the city.* Still, he'd make do. Reed collected a stick of chalk from the shelf then returned to the kitchen, where he set a plate in the sink.

Next came the ash... meaning something had to burn. But not just anything either – failing a branch taken from a living tree, the replacement had to have meaning.

Reed found an old birthday card, placed it in the sink and then rummaged around for a box of matches in the second drawer. They rattled as he lifted them free, only to pause. The card was from a high-school girlfriend, Shannon. It *was* meaningful, but was it enough?

One way to find out.

He struck the match then set the card alight.

Then, he turned to the cupboard and reached up to the back of the shelf for a little set of vials, each one containing about 10mls of his blood. Max and the others always told him it was risky to leave blood lying around, but the building and apartment *were* warded. Heavily.

Next up, chalk. Reed knelt and drew the spidery symbol, a cross between a flower and a web, the blue bright against each white tile. Once the ring of petals and connecting strands were complete, Reed stood and retrieved the warm ashes from his plate.

These he poured into the centre of the symbol before stepping back and chanting softly.

Lights flickered, but only once, and then a thin curl of smoke rose from the ashes, faintly black and yellow... and within, an imp appeared.

Small and typically slender, it was humanoid in shape but bearing more in common with a gecko or lizard. Its eyes sparkled – literally – tiny sparks flickering out to nothing around its face, the bright lights otherwise contained deep within black pools of the imp's pupils.

But the demon's eyes were no celebration. Weaker folk could drown within the eyes, even when it came to one of the 'lesser' creatures bound to Orcus.

The imp spread its webbed hands. "So, this is a bit of a surprise – none of your own family available?" The creature could have been smiling happily. Or menacingly. Or not smiling at all.

"Not really."

The imp shrugged. "Very well, if you've got the blood then I'm your demon. You can call me Turbo. What do you need?"

Reed hesitated.

"What?"

"Ah, it's just–"

"Is there something wrong with my name, is that it? I chose a human one, as is the custom for when we demons visit."

"Well–"

"Because I don't think anyone up here could pronounce my real name."

"Well, it's just that 'turbo' isn't really a name."

"But it means 'fast' doesn't it?"

"Very fast."

"Right, and that's me. Fast."

"Well, that's what I'm looking for. Subtlety and speed," Reed said with a smile.

"Check and check; humans never notice me."

"Perfect." Reed lifted his vial of blood, but kept it in his palm while he outlined the task. "I need you to find the Robert Dunstall that lives here in the city. He's a drug trafficker and is no doubt currently exploiting people in Malaysia."

Turbo paused a moment, then nodded. "I can manage that. Anything else?"

"I need to know his movements for the next few days, since I'm planning to visit him."

"Done. That all?"

"For now, that's enough. Just make sure no-one notices you and that you don't take any side trips or deviate from that task. Standard Contract terms, right?"

"Certainly," he said, his sparkling eyes drifting toward the vial.

Reed lifted the blood to the moonlight – it had turned a deep orange, imbuing the details of the contract, and their bond – then tossed it to the imp. Turbo snatched the vial from the air with a flash, and he really was fast, then drank it down before sighing.

"That's good stuff. You demi-god-types always have a little something extra in there."

"That's… a little gross, Turbo."

"Suppose it is. My turn then," he said, and pierced his forearm, letting pale purple blood drip into the vial. Not much, a mere three drops before he corked it and spoke. "In return, I'll need a room in the city for a single weekend, preferably near some cafes and bars."

"For what purpose?"

"I'm conducting research. I won't even need to leave the hotel room, but I will ask that you arrange things so that I'm not disturbed."

Reed sighed. "I'm going to need more than that."

"I simply need to hear the city, that's all."

"Hear the city?"

"Yes," Turbo said. "Do we have a deal then?"

This is a gamble, but it's worth it... the Contract can't easily be broken. "We do," Reed said. Turbo threw the vial and Reed caught it, removed the stopper, tilted his head back, and let the burning blood strike his tongue.

Chapter 7.

Demon blood sizzled across Reed's tastebuds – biting like citrus and ginger or even the bitterness of apple seeds.

The adrenaline that followed was an unpleasant mix of rage, fear, jealousy and even a hint of arousal. Blessedly, it did not last but such 'vice-juice' as users called it, was a rare item on the black market indeed. Most humans could only tolerate a single drop, and its effects tended to be long-lasting.

And damaging.

"You going to be fine?" Turbo asked.

"No problems," Reed replied after taking a deep breath, leaning on his inhuman side to negate the effect. "When will you need the room?"

"Why not make arrangements while I'm working?"

Reed nodded as he bent by the chalk, to wipe a tile clean. "I'll book now."

"Thank you, partner," Turbo replied, then shot from the web-like symbol and disappeared. The traces of his almost electric energy lingered, and even Reed could sense the tense streams streaking down through the building and into the shadowy streets.

But it soon faded. He was fast indeed.

Reed sighed as he reached for his phone, called the Bourke Street Vantage and made a booking for the weekend. He'd barely finished quoting his credit card details, which were about to get worked over by plane tickets, when a knock echoed from across the room.

Not the door; a gift from his parents, an ornamental koala, was falling to the carpet.

An urchin-like boy – dressed right out of Dickens but cleaner – was shaking his head as he crossed the room. His blond hair gleamed as he looked up.

Conrad.

"Reed, did an imp just race out of here?"

No point lying. "Yes."

"Are you perhaps insane?"

"No. And this isn't my first rodeo; the contract will hold. It's not like I'm some human summoner in over his head."

"We could debate the over your head bit," he replied. "If either of you make a mistake, you'll both pay."

"I know that." *And I have to finish this before Enki returns.*

"Imps are fickle."

"They can be."

Conrad sighed. "Well, here's something else you already know but are choosing not to address – if we make contracts they aren't temporary, like for humans. This 'Turbo' fellow might demand more in the future."

"So might I of him," Reed replied.

"That's not the answer I was hoping for," the seemingly young boy said.

"You reporting back then?" Reed asked.

"Not sure."

"Then Aunty's having me watched, I take it." It should have been at least a small shock... but then, he'd certainly given her plenty of reason not to trust him over the decades. *And she does prefer to sit back and let others do the legwork.*

"You have a real problem with authority figures, don't you?"

Reed stepped into the narrow laundry and grabbed a shovel and brush. "I'm following her rules – I'm not pulling the family into this, and I'm sure you know where things stand with Enki."

"All true," Conrad replied. "Just make sure you don't act rashly, more so… you seem quite angry of late."

"Of late?" Reed paused. "How long have you been watching me?"

"I don't remember." The boy disappeared.

Reed stood, raising his voice. "Keep your eyes to yourself if Emma visits, understood?"

Of course. I am still a gentleman, Reed.

Conrad's voice echoed in his mind.

"Good." Reed finished cleaning up the ash, then broke out the frying pan. *Time for something from childhood.* Ham steaks and pineapple – very 'pub meal'. He also baked some frozen chips for the side, and once he'd eaten, followed it all with fruit salad from a can... not amazing stuff, but sweet and cool at least.

He leant back in his chair and glanced back at the stovetop. *Why am I craving stuff I'd usually eat in the summer?*

Faint vibrations, like an electrical current, filled the room and Turbo stood in the middle of the kitchen once more. "Did you make reservations?"

"On Bourke Street, this weekend. I'll take the key and invite you in."

"Wonderful."

"What about Dunstall? Is he staying put?"

"Actually, he's here in the city; returned a month ago, if I'm judging correctly. No plans for another trip. You can find him at *Club Deity* if you leave soon, since he's taken a room above. Number twelve."

"Oh." A month... had Duong been wrong?

"That's good news, isn't it?" the imp asked.

"It is."

The lizard-like demon nodded its head. "Well then, I'll be off. See you soon, Reed Lavender."

"Wait, why did..." Reed trailed off, Turbo was already gone. *Why did it take him so long?*

And while the link remained in place, there was no way to bring the imp back without a whole new ritual... and Turbo's news was perhaps more interesting. Even if there was no way to know whether he could fully trust the imp about his movements while in the city, the knowledge shared as part of the contract was no lie.

Club Deity – an auspicious name, or an ill omen?

Either way, the owners were about to lose a guest.

Chapter 8.

Club Deity seemed to be 'upmarket sleazy', its neon lights clashing with the fellow in a suit-jacket who appeared more like a doorman than a bouncer. Whether the place doubled as a hotel or a brothel was not clear, but Reed would find out soon enough.

Yet he did not get out of his car.

It wasn't weariness - he'd slept long enough and eaten his fill. Most likely, it was just a trace of the demon blood lingering. *It has to ease up soon.* His muscles twitched, as though eager to lash out. A sharp contrast to Apollo's elixir, where the energy it granted seemed bright and free from any taint.

Rage clung to him, a kind of long tail to the blood's effects, something he had 'bypassed' with his Reaper side, but that which seemed to cling to his human half. *Or maybe it's seeking what's already within me.* But the longer he sat in the car, flicking between radio stations, the more tension locked down his body. *I can't put this off too long.*

Dunstall could leave, or something else could happen. He had to move.

Test your disguise before it's too late.

Reed pulled the door open with a grunt, and swung it closed – harder than he'd intended. But he started across the street at a shuffle, the rage simmering beneath his calm exterior. There was no traffic in the back street, at least, nothing he couldn't dodge as he hunched over in his old coat.

He even affected a raspy cough – going all out on the tricks.

No choice.

Getting in and out of the club was not a problem, precisely, but passing *unrecognised* was important. Dunstall would have powerful friends – they always did, and it was more than likely that at least one of them was connected to the police. And so protecting Duong meant remaining unmarked.

The doorman opened the door with a nod. "Looking to get lucky tonight, old boy?" he asked.

Reed grinned, revealing a few gaps in his teeth as he did, the wrinkles seeming to encroach upon the edges of his very vision. A nice little trick that he didn't like to pull too often – ageing himself was quite risky, but it was an instant change back to 'normal' if he needed it.

Club Deity was dark inside – no surprises there.

The walls seemed to bear paintings but the art was essentially invisible, and pink and blue lights seemed to conceal more than they illuminated, only the glitter of show girls or a white glow from the bar to go by.

The slow burn of the music washed over him, hiding most

of the voices of those in their darkened corners, though anger seemed to lurk within the tone of at least one table.

Reed continued toward the bar, giving a few drunks some room, then groaned as he climbed onto a stool to order. The bartender slid the drink a short distance then turned to another customer.

How to get upstairs next?

Toilets waited off to one side, down a corridor, not too far from what looked like a tiny kitchen. All the way across the room waited a staircase, with a trunk-like bouncer standing guard. Two empty tables rested nearby, being some distance from the stage.

Plan from there.

Reed started across the floor, slow and steady as he gave the waitress and their painted-on tank tops right of way, along with anyone who seemed too drunk to express even the barest shred of consideration for the elderly, and finally, finally he reached the table nearest the stairs.

"Better," he said as he sunk into the chair with his drink, taking a moment to catch his breath. He nearly laughed right after, sounding old certainly came easy enough.

But it didn't solve his problem.

I guess I could try to freak out the guard, take a day or two, rattle him enough to leave? "Hmmm." Too much could go wrong, not to mention, grabbing – and keeping – a hold of the fellow in the first place.

The sound of shattering glass cut through the room.

Shouts followed, and the thudding of furniture against a wall – two or three meatheads scuffling in the shadows. The girls paused but the music continued, and the bouncer charged across the floor.

Reed grinned. *Well, well, some fortune goes my way.*

He rose and started to climb the stairs without looking back. Best to move slow and steady, and by the sounds of things below, he had time.

When Reed reached the top he paused again, gripping the wall a moment. Despite the lingering anger within him, his body simply wasn't up to moving any faster. He glanced down the corridor – just a couple sliding into their room from the shadows, lock clicking firmly after.

"Right." Reed eased up the grip he'd taken on the branches of his own Life Tree, and exhaled as his limbs and spine creaked and cracked, straightening in a flow of something akin to ecstasy. Just to move so freely again, not to ache anymore, a true gift. He shook out a few more kinks, ran a hand over his cheek – not wrinkled now – then pulled his gun before stalking to room number twelve.

With his renewed energy came the anger. *Nearly time now.* He rapped upon Dunstall's door.

"Yes?" A curt voice.

"Your drink, sir," Reed said. *Is that going to be enough?*

"Fine."

You damn fool. Reed opened the door to a lamp-lit room full of cream coloured walls and erotic art. A man lay slouched across a deep couch, his fine suit rumpled and open at the throat; he looked up from a laptop. His hair was turning grey but his face wasn't so lined and eyes were a bright blue.

More importantly, Dunstall was alone.

"Who the fuck are you?" the criminal asked.

Reed levelled his gun at the pig, whose eyes widened. "I have a better question – do you want to leave with a limp, or walk out on both legs?"

He set the laptop aside but did not rise. "Who are you and how the hell did you know I was here?"

"Sounds like one leg to me." Reed pulled a silencer from his coat pocket. Dramatic, yes, but it was supposed to intimidate. Yet so far, Dunstall didn't seem too off-balance. Concerned, but not panicked. "Want to change your answer?"

"What is this about?"

"A girl. You ordered Froud to shut her up, she wasn't working out."

"You're a whack-job, aren't you?" Dunstall said. "I have no idea what you're on about, but you should leave if you know what's good for you."

"Care to repeat that threat?" Reed produced his phone, and hit the record button. "Look, Dunstall. If you confess, you will feel better. And I might not take little your enterprise down either."

Dunstall's frown deepened. *Finally some visible concern.* "Who are you?"

"Someone who knows the truth." Reed tapped to pause the recording. "And your executioner if you don't speak up."

The drug lord folded his arms. "You're going to murder me here? For what? Justice, for some silly little bitch in over her head? I gave her one chance too many before I told Froud what to do."

There it was.

"And if this was legit, buddy, then you'd be here with a warrant, which you're not. You need me alive to confess again, so you're not killing me, we both know that."

Anger stirred. "Do you?"

"I do, shit-face," Dunstall leered. "And you know what, you've shown your face so not only do I *know* this isn't anything more than a scare tactic, but I can describe you quite accurately to the police, which will probably be a first for me."

"Think you can talk from beyond the grave?"

"Give it up!" the man snapped. "What are you, some private detective on his first job? You didn't think this through – and you should have, especially if you know who I am, and if you found me here. Because now, whatever friend you have that tipped you off, well, you just got them killed too."

"Too?"

"Yeah."

Reed shook his head. "Your confidence is something else, Dunstall."

He laughed. "Why shouldn't it be? I could tell you exactly what you wanted to hear, even say it for your phone if you turn the recording back on, and you could take it to the police. Know what would happen?"

"What?"

"Sweet fuck all – I own enough of them, so you know what? You'd be the one in jail, if you're lucky."

Now Reed grinned, though it strained his cheeks. "I'm already in jail."

"Are you fucking high?"

"Not yet." But maybe the bastard was right. *Maybe rushing in was a mistake – but I couldn't do this as an old timer.* Whatever wound up on tape, and he had plenty of material on a second recording device hidden in his shirt, wasn't going to mean shit if Dunstall shut down an investigation.

Which might lead to Duong getting hurt after all...

And would mean, that for the thousandth time, he'd failed Elise.

No way.

Reed clenched his teeth.

Dunstall glared as he stood, jabbing a finger toward Reed. "Now it's time for *you* to make a decision. Are you going to leave now? Take a head start? Or maybe wait here for my friends to visit you?"

"No."

"There ain't no third option," he said with a smirk.

Reed lowered his gun, a tingle of demon blood almost singeing his tongue, the simmering anger boiling over. Darkness narrowed his vision down Dunstall's stupid fucking face.

"Well, dipshit?"

Reed clicked off his tape, as though merely rubbing at his chest.

He leapt forward.

Dunstall staggered back, stumbling onto the couch as Reed crashed into the man, clawing for his throat. The drug-baron thrashed about, beating at Reed's hands but he only squeezed harder.

Already his hands were bones.

He hissed then, smashing his way through the man's pupils and tearing at the branches of a greying Lifespan tree. With each leaf and limb he tore, Reed heard – and ignored – a plea for help. It was no voice from Dunstall's crushed windpipe, more a screech from the man's soul.

But it meant nothing.

Just like it meant nothing to the fucker when he

ordered Elise's life ended.

Reed kept snapping branches, taking days, weeks and years, decades even – until too fast, he'd reached the base of the already sickened tree. And still Dunstall struggled, weakening now.

But it was all for nothing. Reed tore the final branch free, a strip of bark slicing free with it, and Dunstall fell still beneath his grip.

Silence roared across the room.

Reed blinked until the sound of blood rushing to his ears returned, the rasp of his breath or the creak of his bones, the white faded as skin tones reappeared upon his hands. "I did it," Reed said with a shudder, falling back onto the couch beside the corpse.

The man behind Elise's murder was dead. Justice had been served.

"Yes you did, sadly."

Conrad stood in the corner of the room.

Chapter 9.

"You shouldn't have broken that rule, Reed," the small Reaper said. His newsboy cap was slightly askew but it did not cover his eyes – expression mournful rather than angry. "You know that, you great fool."

"Elise has justice now."

"No, you took your vengeance."

Reed climbed to his feet, but his legs trembled. He slumped back against the cushions, where he shoved at Dunstall's corpse. "I recorded it all, he admitted it. I'm getting both."

"If you stay here, you're getting a murder charge."

"Heart failure, that's all they'll find in the autopsy."

"Reed!"

"You didn't stop me."

Conrad stamped a foot, the sound soft against the carpet. "That's not my job."

"Just paid to watch, huh?"

His cousin appeared beside him. "And take you to Aunty." Conrad's small hand fell upon Reed's shoulder and then the walls of room twelve were gone.

Instead, Reed found himself upright, walking a quiet gallery.

He had lost control of his limbs and it was already difficult to recall where he'd been moments ago. The clean white walls of the gallery were tinted orange by a non-existent sunset... since there were no windows. Instead, figures robed in black sat before ornate frames of gold, each canvas blank. But the painters worked nevertheless, dipping brushes into the rainbow of colours upon their palettes.

The nearest fellow dipped his brush into the green but when he moved his hand, no line of colour appeared on his canvas.

"Excuse me?" Reed spoke softly as he neared.

The painter turned, revealing an open robe.

A line of green paint was visible upon his chest. *The stroke he just made a moment ago?* The fellow's face was composed but he did not seem to see Reed, returning to his work.

And for his own part, Reed's feet bore him on past the painter, past each of them, as he strode through similar halls. In each corridor, the amount of artists and the size of their canvases eventually grew smaller. *This has to lead to something.*

It was not a building he'd ever visited when it came to Death's mansion.

And now he was walking faster, heading to a long hall – a hall that seemed familiar for the echoes of the human world, a hall built to offer room to really take in the statue waiting at its end... a place somewhat similar to where David stood in the Uffizi Gallery, but this was no Michelangelo work of art.

A robed shape towered over Reed; onyx shot through

with flaming white lines like marble... twin staves, each bearing a blank face, same as the one in the centre. The force of its very presence driving him to his hands and knees, even forcing his head down so that he saw only polished floorboards.

Mors, Goddess of Death.

You have broken my Laws. Do you confess to this?

"Yes."

Others have come to speak for you, but I will determine your eternity: you will work here, cataloguing the deaths of all living things non-human. Failing that, you will Dive the Sands.

Reed flinched.

Not that!

Diving the Sands was not something meant for humans, or half Reapers either – few children of Death tolerated it for very long. It was mostly used as a punishment.

Painting for an eternity, that would be *far* more acceptable, an entirely different punishment... and perhaps, knowing that Dunstall was dead, knowing that he'd kept his promise to Elise, perhaps he could bear the gallery until, just maybe, he could be forgiven. But Diving was *not the same*.

Reed began to tremble.

Regret mingled with his fear. *My body.* In a sense, his body would not survive the gallery in any meaningful way. And it also meant that no-one would find the recording of Dunstall. *A chance at true justice for Elise.*

Conrad had been right, vengeance had taken over his mind. Maybe he could argue to himself that the demon blood pushed him along, but it hadn't encouraged anything that wasn't already within him.

Let them speak.

"It is *possible* that the demon's blood drove him beyond what he might have done without it?" Conrad, as though reading Reed's mind.

Not a ringing endorsement, but better than nothing.

Reed couldn't look up to see who else had come to speak, but surely Max and Lina at least?

"Reed and his parents are connected to the Radiant King, we need him in more ways than one," Max said.

Better – logic would appeal to Aunty.

"He helps us understand humans," Lina announced. "Katarina is not so generous with her time."

Katarina? Who was that? Another half-skull?

"He owes debts to many," said a new voice, an older woman speaking – Magdalena, who he had not seen since he was a child. "He ought to have a chance to repay them."

"Jupiter sees value in him." This time, it was a voice he did not recognise.

More voices came, other cousins, other relatives with young and old voices alike, all offering dry and logical reasons, reasons attached to utility and function. Nothing personal, and though that came as no surprise, Reed could not help feel the sting.

"He answers every call." A soothing voice, offering the impression of a more sincere or gentler preacher. Was that...?

Reed tried to raise his head but still, he could not move.

No voices followed, and it seemed that the last had been Somnus? Mors' own brother had come to speak for him? Reed drew in a breath. Maybe there was a chance?

Your words have been noted, all. Mors announced. *Let it be known that Katarina will operate in his stead and I will clear all debts. Finally, you can all agree – the Law is inviolate; he is sentenced to the Sands.*

Chapter 10.

Time was a river of sand. It swirled with grains of light, grains of silvery shadow too – all somewhat meaningless as it surrounded him, pressed in on him, even when he slept, even when he wasn't actually diving.

Even now.

Reed stood in a mighty crater upon a dark... moon, it seemed, any ceiling or sky lost in shadow, save for the glimmering torrent of sand that poured down endlessly to the pile below.

Like the peak of an hourglass, the monstrous mound of sand did not change in size or shape, but nor did the sand stop. It rained down, grains escaping to hang beside the stream, a golden haze in the air.

Yet every piece – every soul – still found its way to the bottom sooner or later.

These were the lives that had not been recycled... for various reasons. All were stored here, waiting to be reused. Only, most proved unsuitable in some manner. Many returned quickly, just as often they were *returned* by Reapers.

These were not the kind of people – monsters – that Reed wished to meet, let alone wrangle.

Yet he had no choice.

Even the 'good' ones did not provide enjoyable meetings... or maybe his heart simply wasn't large enough to cope? To care so much, so often and so long.

The elongated, floating bone beside him, not unlike a luminous fox skull, gestured to the rail and the silver thread.

"This is all a little unsophisticated, isn't it?" Reed asked.

Of course, like each day, the skull did not answer. But it was no empty vessel either, for it could compel him to act and it did *something* to dampen emotions. That much was clear, but even so, the souls he sought out still struck him. *If the fox didn't help, I wouldn't have lasted this long.* However long 'long' was. But again, measuring time was impossible – no change in light, little change in routine, just diving, chasing, retrieving and resting. It wasn't sleep either, just a period of 'not diving' which he could not count.

Anger had drained away, bitter regret left in its place.

Returning to the world above seemed impossible, yet the tainted hope he repressed would not let him abandon the idea. Wasn't there a chance, no matter how tiny, that Max and Lina were working on something? Was Emma safe?

The city itself?

And the Radiant King still had to be stopped, if he wasn't already loose again.

The fox urged Reed forward. "I know, I know."

He glanced around before he took the rope; four other Reapers with their own glowing fox skulls approached the rails and dove, the silvery tethers bright where they spiralled down from storeys above and below.

Reed took his own thread and braced himself.

The silver pierced his chest, questing past his organs to lock into his spine. The thread also gave him a target: a single grain within the mountain. This time, a woman whose last twelve lives had ended in suicide. She'd appear as a bright blue grain, but like most of the others, she'd hide. For a soul like her, she'd probably run, desperate not to return. Plead and beg. Maybe scream.

And he would have to bear it all, ignore her terror.

Drag her back to the world in Aunty's name.

Reed climbed onto the rail then leapt for the pile, scowling the whole way down. When he smashed into the sand it offered no shockwave. Instead, he slipped easily into a shimmering darkness, warm but empty despite what should have been a weight above him.

His dive sent him deep, deep enough that he didn't have to kick or swim at first.

Around him, vague in the unclear distance, the sense of other divers, but never had he actually crossed paths with one.

A wink of blue.

Reed twisted, kicking to the left.

It darted ahead, moving fast – but not so fast that he couldn't keep up. Reed bore down on the single grain of sand, reaching out. It skipped and twisted, twirled out of his grasp and he kicked harder. And harder, stretching so that his muscles strained – and then his hand closed over the soul, flicking into his palm as if called by magnets.

His dive came to a halt.

Darkness followed, until a room of blue resolved from the ink and in it a woman with lovely curls sat upon a bed, her gaze despondent.

"Do not take me, please."

"I must."

"That's a lie," she said. "You're different from the others."

"I don't have a choice," he said.

She shook her head. "No, *I* don't have a choice."

Is she right about that? The first few times the fox had compelled him when he'd refused to dive, something that had been... unpleasant. Reed stepped forward, he held out a hand. "Maybe this time will be–"

"No!" she sprang to her feet. "Don't say it – this time *won't* be different. We both know that. There's obviously something wrong with me if I keep ending up here! Why can't you see that?" She was crying now. "Why send me back when you know exactly what will happen? Do you sick fucks like seeing me suffer?"

Reed flinched. "I don't know what will happen when you go back, but I know nothing will change for the better if you stay here."

She spat. "I do. Everything will be exactly the same. Everything! And the worst thing is that I won't have a fucking clue when I get up there. I won't remember any of this, won't remember the last twelve times and when the same hopelessness takes over I'll end up here sooner or later."

"What if this is the time to break the cycle?"

She slumped back onto the bed, laughing a flat, empty laugh. "Sure thing, buddy."

Reed moved closer – when souls lashed out it could get

painful – then put a hand on her shoulder. "I want this to be the time you find happiness."

She looked up at him, eyes still void of hope. "Why don't they help me?"

Reed found himself back in his cell of stone, windowless but not dark somehow.

Silence, coolness and the inability to move. *Just like the time before, and the time before that.* Supposedly, time to rest – but his chest ached and his throat was closing up already as tears built. Something of her despair remained, working its way into him.

Or maybe it was her question that lingered?

Had she been asking about *people* above, or the gods who set her soul loose once more?

"Fox!" he called.

Its mere presence would dull his emotion but it didn't always come at once.

He called again, and a new figure appeared.

Potter.

Reed blinked. *Potter* stood in the doorway. The man carried no scythe and his hood had been pulled back, revealing his classically handsome but exceedingly pale face, head smooth and bald. "Reed."

"I didn't expect to see you, Potter."

"Of course."

"So, have you come to gloat about my punishment, then?"

"No," he replied, his frown deep as he entered the cell. "I am here to intercede on your behalf."

Reed sat up – and he actually *could* sit up. "You?"

"I have need of your talents."

"So you're here to blackmail me." Hardly a generous

response, but the words slipped out. And it made sense. *Even if he's the last person I expected to turn up here, doesn't mean his motives are pure.* But hope stirred within nevertheless. "I don't understand this."

"An exchange is not blackmail."

"You've convinced Mors to relent but I have to do something for you?"

"No."

Reed stood to speak now, but the luminous fox skull appeared behind Potter. The Reaper flicked a gesture over his shoulder, and the skull melted back into the shadowy hall. "This is... outside of Mother's province."

"You're going behind her back? Breaking her rules?"

Potter folded his arms. "That is what you have never seemed to understand. Mother *is* the rule of death. It is hard for her to see beyond those vital structures."

"But you do."

"I am afforded more flexibility, yes."

Reed couldn't help a shake of his head. "I've never heard you say anything remotely close to such a thing. What's going on?"

Potter held his gaze a moment. "We will talk once you are elsewhere."

"How? Aunty will know every step we take."

"I will incur her wrath in this, but she will come to see what is necessary."

What in all the hells am I about to get myself into? "I don't think I have a choice, do I?"

"You do. You can in fact stay here and continue to dive for eternity. I will find another."

"Let's go."

Chapter 11.

Potter sat across from Reed in a bright dining hall of white and gold, of lamps shaped like fountains; steady, pulsating glows. The hall, and the palace it sat within, had been built upon an enormous ship – far too enormous to rock within whatever body of water it rested upon. In fact, the marble, mosaic floors and indoor plumbing suggested something unlikely. *On the other hand, why not?*

"You seem to recognise this place," Potter said.

"Based on the size and structures alone, what you've shown me is like a floating palace... Like the Nemi ships. Maybe bigger – but I thought the hulls were destroyed in World War II?"

"Indeed, this is one of Caligula's mighty pleasure barges. I have restored and expanded it somewhat, though I have a far more sedate use for it. Certainly we are not floating upon Lake Nemi either."

Reed glanced around again. Heavy velvet curtains of dark purple, almost black, flanked pastoral frescos and in the corners, slender, sculpted cypress trees all shaped as warriors and perhaps other gods, many he did not recognise.

More surprising however, was the revelation that Potter actually possessed a personality. "I didn't expect all this."

"Your honesty is welcome."

And it was impressive – all of it. Reed couldn't deny an urge to explore more of the place, but there *were* more pressing matters to deal with. "Now that I'm free, I have to thank you. And ask, what's going on?"

Potter nodded. "It is Enki. I am growing to suspect something, especially considering the news you and the younglings brought."

"Younglings?"

"Such is my right, as one of the eldest," Potter replied, with a slight frown. "To return to the matter before us, Enki was once known as a God of Creation and Knowledge, of Water and also Mischief. His reign was in prehistoric times though how he faded is not clear, even to us. But I sense something in his return, something in his trials beneath your city."

"He's putting humans through test-runs, I think. Both Dad and Mum were taken for that purpose, I know that much."

"So it seems, sadly," Potter said and his voice almost seemed to express regret. "In his union with Feronia, and with the knowledge he slowly gleans, I believe Enki will eventually create a fully functioning city of this Parginos. With it, he will supplant Melbourne and eventually the entire continent, and given enough time, beyond."

"The whole country and beyond?" Troubling as it all was – and it *was* troubling – what precisely did Potter have in mind to counter such a threat? *Can he even do anything against that? Or maybe,* why *is he getting involved like this?*

"Yes."

"But, would that really change things for you? If Parginos still has human, animal and plant life, then you will still have a purpose, right?"

"Not in Enki's plan. He will be supreme here."

"Is that even possible?"

"If no-one stops him, it is indeed possible."

Reed leant across the pristine tablecloth. "But the Gods would simply band together, surely? Especially if he's still Returning, Enki's no match for the combined might of–"

Potter raised a hand. "They speak quite openly now, of a new playground should this one continue to hold no more surprises for them."

"Wait..." *They'd actually abandon us?* But then, hadn't Max mentioned something similar at one point? "They wouldn't just give the earth away."

"Jupiter arranged for us to work against Enki via our agents, as you know. Considering the link to your parents, you are vital to that resistance."

He nodded slowly. "And having me stuck Diving the Sands helps no-one."

"Of course."

Reed chuckled, though no mirth warmed his heart. "I find myself utterly unsurprised. And equally furious." *Typical of the Gods and their skewed concept of life. And death. And time, for that matter.*

"I expect you will use that spirited stubbornness of yours for what is to come."

He nodded. "How?"

"Not unlike before: marshal your talents and allies in order to stop Enki before he succeeds in finishing Parginos."

"That simple?"

"It is my hope, yes." Potter gestured to their surroundings with a pale hand. "I have grown accustomed to many things here. I do not wish to give them up and start again, with the bickering and the vying for roles and dominion."

Again, the image of Potter as a strictly dull enforcer of rules took a bit of a battering. "What about Aunty?"

"As I and others ask you to gamble your life, so I must do the same."

"What do you mean?"

"Hide and seek."

"Ah...?"

Potter almost smiled. "Did you not play that once as a child? Hiding from your young human friends or even adults? Teachers perhaps, during school?"

"I did, but I'm still not sure what you're getting at."

"So any child might deceive, Reed, even the child of a god. And so that is what I propose; a vital game of hide and seek."

"I've never been able to hide from the gods – if they want to find me, they do."

"Correct." Potter stood and removed his black robe, revealing a sculpted body, not unlike a marble statue. He folded the robe and slid it across the empty dining table. "And that is why you will assume my mantle."

Chapter 12.

"There are several mirrors within the hanging garden," Potter said. "You can see what others will see."

Reed lifted the heavy robes, arm straining. *What is this?* The weight of what had to be at least an eternity of unfulfilled hopes and dreams pressed against him, none specific but none so vague that couldn't remember the anguish as though it was his own.

He fell to his knees with a cry – it seemed to escape like a bird taking flight.

"It does not last."

"How?"

"How what?"

"How do you bear this each time?"

"Wear it and you will see. It does not last."

Reed slid an arm within, the despair vanished. The mantle was light and warm, yet the sense that it would be perfectly suitable for a desert came to him as well. And now, so soon after the hopelessness, a feeling of safety settled across him too, like the cloth was the strongest armour.

This I certainly prefer. "What was that?"

"A reminder."

"You face that each time you dress?"

"Admittedly, I rarely remove the robes but when I do, it is important to recall the gravity of my role," he said, and a frown appeared. "Something I believe you must still learn in full."

Ah, the old Potter returns. "You're referring to Lily?"

"Perhaps. But that is not our concern today. I must inform you; with my robe you will be much closer to a true Reaper, so manage your anger well. It will also allow you to pass unseen of a night, though not so perfectly in the day. I have granted other, minor boons but those are the two you should be aware of for now."

"This is impressive, Potter," Reed said, and it was nothing he'd expected either. "But, can we really pull this off? Will the family mistake me for you, when I'm out there?"

"Few would be able to see through what I have woven, but you must act the part. And worry not, for if any do see you, and they then choose to seek me thereafter, they will fail. Even Mother," he said, tone offering no hint of doubt.

"What if they send Aunty my way instead?"

"You will have to get creative."

"Thanks."

"To offer my honesty, Reed, she will be more concerned about me, and so you should be able to manipulate her thusly. *I* am the one who has broken her edict, and I am the one she will seek."

More old-school Potter. But in the end, it was better than Diving. "I can't argue with that. Let's see how I look, then."

Reed strode from the dining hall and into a long

corridor, with regular branching passages, each dotted by tall, narrow trees and to the hanging garden they'd passed earlier. There, he found one of the mirrors – it had been arranged to reflect the potted plants and their cascading flowers – but Reed saw only his new face. Unsmiling, an intense gaze, a tint of blue to the skin. A faint shiver followed.

I even look taller.

"This is unnerving."

The real, naked marble Potter raised a thin eyebrow. "I did not think I was so unpleasant to look upon."

"You're not; it'll just take a bit of adjusting, is all."

"Then do so as swiftly as you can," he said with a nod, then snapped his fingers. A grey line appeared in the fabric of the garden, heat from the Fringe emanating. "Pass through. You will find the Fringe far more tolerable so long as you wear the robe."

"This leads home, I take it?"

"Yes."

"Where will you be, if I need your help?"

The man actually chuckled, a flat sound. "Best that you do not know. And Reed, you *are* receiving my help right now. Do not waste all that I have arranged here."

Reed raised a hand to forestall a lecture. "Fair enough."

"Once you return, gather those you feel will help. They may respond quicker to a call that appears to come from me."

"Even people like Sirius?" *That would be something; Sirius was a powerhouse but somewhat fickle.*

"I believe so," he replied. "Now go, I still have things to attend to."

Reed nodded as he strode to the Fringe, but with one foot within, he paused to look back. "Thank you."

"Of course."

The grey waste of the Fringe was far less 'waste-like' with his first few steps across the decks of the Nemi ship. The shadows were deeper and when he reached the rail, Reed found that the ship rested upon a field of snow... or so it seemed. Heat rushed up to meet him, but the robe deflected it while keeping him aware of what lay beyond.

A second tear in the air itself waited at the rail and when he stepped through, it was to stumble into the shadows of his own living room – where Max and Lina sat cross-legged before his television. They were pointing and laughing as they passed a bucket of fried chicken between them.

"What are you doing?" Reed asked.

Max frowned. "Potter?"

"We're watching a fashion show," Lina said. "We got your message. So, where's Reed?"

Reed removed the robe. "I'm here."

Max half-rose, then slumped back down, eyes wide. "So much for following Mother's rules, I see."

"Believe it or not, this was Potter's idea," Reed said. He pointed to the television. "And how often do you do this sort of thing when I'm out? Or is it only when I'm condemned to Dive the Sands for eternity?"

Lina sprang up to spin into a graceful – but entirely insincere – curtsey. "Sorry, cousin."

"Uh-huh."

She smiled, her blue-painted lips taking on a brightness in the TV's glow. "It's still nice to have you back, you know. We'd been working on Mother, but to no avail."

"Well, let's keep her out of this for now," Reed said,

explaining his visit with Potter. "There are a couple of things I want to do before we head back down there."

"Checking up on Emma?" Max asked. "She recovered just fine too."

"Did you tell her what happened?" Reed began to gather his things, keys, wallet and phone – who had gathered them and from where? *Maybe it doesn't matter, so long as I've got them again.* "How long have I been gone?"

"Only a week, give or take. We actually spent a lot longer in Parginos, as time moves here, at least."

Reed paused, phone in hand. *Hadn't it said 'November' before?* "So, what's the date?"

"Not sure, but it's summer, if that helps."

"Not really."

"Like I said before, plenty of unknowns about Enki and his city."

Lina nodded. "It really is an interesting place."

"Ah, can we shift focus a bit?" Reed asked. "While I visit Emma, why don't you two try Terra. She's pretty old, so maybe she'll know something about Enki?"

"Conrad and Clio are already seeking Minerva's help with that task, but you know how the old girl is, not much of a talker nowadays."

"Emma too," Lina added. "She's really thrown herself into the search, now that she has all that free time."

Reed winced. "Free time?"

"Yeah. She lost her job after her family filed a missing persons' report."

"Oh, shit," Reed snatched up Potter's robe, flinching at the wave of regret that caused him to stumble. *I hope this fades soon.* But he strode for the door as he pulled it on, and called over his shoulder from the hallway. "You know where I'll be if you get any news."

But he'd only made it to the dimly lit elevator when Lina appeared – just her face on the 'down' button. "Remember that officer you lied to?"

"Huggins."

"Well, between he and Duong, they're *very* confused, since you're still in solitary confinement. I think it's making a bit of trouble for them still, especially with the body of that drug-dealer you left in the club."

"Ah." *That's going to be a problem.* "So the doll's still holding up?"

"Of course."

"I'll figure something out," he said, leaning against the wall. Though no ideas came to mind; it wasn't much easier to solve than the problem of Enki. But if he could just make sure Emma was okay first...

As the elevator slowed, Reed whipped Potter's robe across his shoulders and strode across the lobby. It was brighter than the elevator but the night receptionist did not seem to notice any movement as Reed exited, either due to the man's sleepiness or Potter's robe.

Either way, Reed found himself striding for the nearest taxi rank – which wasn't near at all. The night certainly wasn't cold, and flashing lights and thudding music from more than one party kept him company as much as his thoughts.

Somehow, losing an entire season didn't seem so bad, even if his body and mind were still catching up.

Anything's better than the Sands.

Chapter 13.

Reed knocked upon Emma's door and waited. When no-one answered he knocked again, then turned to large glass windows that overlooked the river, golden highlights on black water. *Far prettier than the muddy green of day. And far nicer than her last place too.*

Reed caught his reflection. "Whoops." He glanced up and down the hall – no-one else around – then removed his robe, folding it over one arm. Emma probably wouldn't even have seen him if she'd answered right then? He pulled out his phone to dial her number, wincing at the midnight hour – but she answered quickly, raising her voice a little over some music, something that sounded like *The Pixies*.

"Reed!"

"I'm right outside; I wanted to check on you."

"On my way, hold on."

Reed hung up in time for the door to open, revealing a smiling Emma. She wore pyjama shorts and a shapeless t-shirt that half-snagged an arm as she leapt forward to hug him. "Reed."

He smiled back. "Hey."

"Max and Lina told me they'd get you back somehow... but I was starting to get worried."

"Guess I got lucky." He lowered his head a little to kiss her. His own relief at her recovery lent a bit of urgency and she kissed him back, reaching up to his face.

"Hold that thought," she said. "I want to show you something inside."

"Deal."

Reed followed her into the apartment – spacious, with the open-plan look that barely suggested separate rooms – but it was gleaming with chrome and clean white surfaces – those that weren't covered in books, maps and notepads, anyway. Emma had turned the music down and was settling back onto one of the stools by the kitchen bench, clicking at her laptop, her other hand sliding him a tablet. "Look at this."

Reed lifted it. A catalogue page showed a single image, a picture of a sequence of notes. Twelve only, faintly drawn on ancient paper. He squinted. *I shouldn't have given up on learning to read music.* "These seem a little discordant, to be honest."

"Well, it *could* be something like the song I mentioned before we went beneath the city, the one villagers used to banish the skin demon, remember?"

"Really?"

"No way to be sure until we try it out, I suppose," she said, then gestured to his robe. "Isn't that a bit much for this weather?"

"Well, there's a story behind it," he said, looking around for a spot to put it aside, and settling on an armchair. "This is a really nice place."

"And you're wondering how I can afford it, after losing my job?"

He spread his hands. "Actually, I came to make sure you were okay. I feel responsible for that, if you hadn't have–"

"It's fine, really." Emma pushed some of her research to one side then gestured to the stool beside her. "Want some coffee?"

"That's how you're staying up so late each night?"

She shrugged. "Maybe. You want some or not?"

"Why not? Double the milk though."

"I know."

Reed glanced down at the research. Various notes around Enki and others, Ea and Anu, Nammu, Ninhursag and others he could not place. The number forty was also underlined. "Max and Lina said you were hard at work. Found anything?"

"Not a whole lot aside from the song. I've been trying to verify its links to Mesopotamia but it's not easy. I'm waiting on some documents from Minerva, actually."

"What about the number forty?"

"Ah, a sacred number for Enki," Emma said from where she prepared their drinks. "But I haven't been able to discover if it can help us yet."

"I guess the song is most important, then?" Reed said. "Especially if we can use the Sonorous and other Bells."

"I'm thinking so."

"So, what about your job?" Reed said as he leant forward.

"The library is going to find a way, hopefully before the contract of the guy who replaced me is up," she said, raising her voice over the boiling kettle. "In the meantime, I get to stay here and work on Enki and Parginos."

"The State Library is paying for this place?"

"No, that'd be my father – out of guilt or relief, I don't know."

"Oh."

Emma finished up and handed him his coffee. "I know it's wrong to take his money, but you know what? He can afford it, Reed. And it's only until I get steady work again."

"Sorry." He raised both hands. "That wasn't supposed to sound like I was judging. So, what did you tell everyone?"

"Well, I think that's part of the 'guilt' thing, you know." She took a sip. "When Lina picked me up from Apollo, I wasn't fully conscious and it seems like your cousin did all the talking when she dropped me off."

"Oh no."

"Right. She told the police that I'd been abducted."

"What?"

"I know. It was all semi-probable, at least, or the way she told it must have been convincing, because when I woke in the hospital for tests, everyone I saw had already accepted the story."

"Well, it's mostly worked out, I guess."

She nodded. "What about you? What happened?"

Reed explained, glossing over a few details, but from a slight pursing of her lips, it seemed she'd press him sooner or later. "I'm fine now, really. We still have to figure out what to do about Enki and Parginos."

"Optimistic."

"Well, maybe not before tomorrow," he said. Despite the caffeine hit, Reed found himself blinking a little too often. *Well. That crept up on me.*

"You can take a shower if you like," she said, and

hesitated. "I think maybe I'm going to do a little more work though."

"Thanks." He nodded as he rose to take his mug to the sink, but stopped. "Wait a minute."

"What's wrong?"

You idiot, this is risky. "I don't know if this is safe, you know, maybe I shouldn't be here."

"Why not?" She set her own coffee down. "Haven't you and Max and Lina worked everything out?"

"Not precisely. Potter busted me out and Aunty doesn't know. I doubt she's looking for me... maybe I should sleep in the robe, just in case."

"The robe? Why?"

"It's a disguise. It'll seem like I'm Potter if I wear it... although, that doesn't solve the potential problem of Enki. He could have agents, just like us. Maybe I should go home, I've got wards up there and I'll be closer to the cemetery–"

Emma took him by the shoulders. "Slow down. Just stay here, Reed. Minerva has blessed this place herself, all right? Nothing's sneaking up on us."

Welcome news indeed. "In that case, are you sure you don't need a shower too?"

Chapter 14.

Reed parked in the shade of the manicured gardens in the Melbourne General Cemetery's car park and dialled Irene Roberts, winding the window down for air as he waited. Heat carried the sound of cicadas en masse along with it, but despite the temperature Reed didn't rush for the air-conditioning.

He even tapped his fingers on the steering wheel. *Shit, I actually think I'm feeling good.* While down in Parginos, someone in the family had sorted the repairs and insurance and so now his car was all fixed up; sitting in the old driver's seat again was like a warm memory. He'd also escaped the Sands *and* winter at the same time, gaining Potter as a powerful ally.

Things really are going well with Emma too.

And on top of everything, finally, he was able to deliver good news for a change.

The weight of the remaining problems seemed... not lighter, but at least more manageable. *The truth about Mum and Dad.* Enki still had to be stopped too, and Patrick rescued, but maybe, if everyone worked together, there was a chance.

"Hello?"

"Mrs Roberts, it's Reed Lavender."

"Mr Lavender, I'm happy to hear from you. I had a feeling, you know, it had been so long."

"I'm sorry about that, but I do have some news at last, Irene. I found the truth – Robert Dunstall, the man who ordered the murder of your granddaughter, has admitted to the crime."

"Really? Oh." A shuddering, indrawn breath followed her query and it took her a moment to continue. "Thank you, dear. Tell me – he'll go to prison, won't he, this Dunstall?"

"He actually died of heart failure." Reed hesitated. "I'm sorry that he won't face justice."

"No," she replied softly. "He took my granddaughter away... that doesn't make him deserving of life in my book. I'll be sure to send along something extra, Mr Lavender."

"Oh, I couldn't accept any more payment. What we agreed upon was fair."

"Now, now. Don't deny me this pleasure, you earned it."

He smiled. "Thank you, Irene."

"Be proud. You've brightened my day and I hope yours is the same. And keep an eye on the post, won't you?" she said as she made her goodbyes.

Reed lowered his phone, still smiling. "I will."

Time to deliver the news one more time.

He took the white rose he'd brought and climbed out of the car, starting along the carefully maintained paths. They were wide enough for pedestrian or car, with extremely gentle speed limits.

Of course he kept the black robe slung across one arm, since traipsing around in such an outfit in a cemetery would have been in poor taste, even if mostly invisible. In the daylight, the robe wouldn't work perfectly and if someone caught a glimpse of a shadowy figure...

He passed more than a few people, offering just a nod or sometimes a smile. Some were holding back tears, some very quietly moving away from headstones or plaques, while a few spoke together softly as they guided small children.

At Elise's grave he placed the rose then knelt in the warm grass. "I'm sorry you had to wait so long for me to keep my promise."

He paused. *Whether she can hear this or not, I have to say it aloud. Maybe later, I can get someone to pass on a message... after all, I've broken all the other rules.*

"They're both dead but I don't know – I never knew – if that's what you wanted or not. I did it for me, as much as you, I guess. At least they can't do anything like that again. That much I managed." He sighed. "But you know what, to hell with those pieces of shit. I should be talking about you. I know you missed a lot of things that we adults take for granted, stuff we think is just normal, stuff we expect will happen... and you should have had a chance to find those things. I hope that next time, after you've passed through the Wheel, that you'll be lucky enough."

He stood but did not leave right away.

A weight had been lifted... but most of that seemed to have come from speaking with Irene. *Maybe that shouldn't be a surprise.*

"Reed Lavender. Just what the fuck is going on here?"

Duong stood upon the path, arms folded, eyes narrowed. Smoke rose from a cigarette in his mouth, and he held the pack in one hand. His blue shirt was open at the throat and his slacks were creased, as though he'd been on a stakeout... which obviously he had.

"It's a cemetery."

He flicked his cigarette to the ground and stomped on it. "Very funny. Tell me what's going on. Apparently I've got your bloody body double in a psych ward, one that's only spoken a few dozen words in *months*, and now I see you out here?"

A fair question – and damn it, I don't have an answer for him either. I should have worn the robe after all. But when did they transfer me? "That's not something I can explain."

"Try."

Shit. "Are you safe, Duong? I mean, can you trust the people above you?"

"Maybe. But only because things cooled off once Dunstall kicked the bucket. They're happy enough because they think you're basically comatose in a psychiatric hospital," he said, lighting another cigarette. "This have anything to do with the answers you owe me?"

"Well, it sounds like you're going to have to keep my secret a little longer to stay out of their sights." *I'll need Lina for this. Shit, I need time to think.*

"Are you telling me you conned everyone in order to get transferred to a psychiatric hospital and that you somehow escaped without being seen on camera? Twice! From a police station *and* a secure ward?"

"I don't know about the cameras, but I'm here, aren't I?"

"Reed."

He sighed. "Look, walk me back to the car and I'll tell you some things."

"Fine."

"Do you ever think about the true nature of the world? Like, what humanity knows and what it only *thinks* it knows? Stuff like that?"

Duong frowned. "This going somewhere?"

"I hope so. Can you answer the question?"

"Not often, no," he replied. "But it sounds like you're about to pitch a religion."

"Nothing so shady. How about this then – do you think humanity has figured it all out already? That we know everything about the world and the universe, life and death?"

"Not a chance," he replied, taking a long drag. "Get to the point, Reed. Tell me how this relates to what's been going on."

He glanced at the detective. "I want to show you something that won't make sense, and I don't know how you'll react."

"And when I see this thing I'll understand how you pulled off your escape?"

"You will," Reed said. "But it might make things worse."

Duong stopped. "Worse how?"

"Follow me." Reed led him to a pair of elms then took a deep breath. *This* never *goes well and you always get chewed out for trying.* But he had to do something. "I want you to meet someone first."

"Who?"

"My cousin."

He stomped on another cigarette. "Your cousin is in

this cemetery, just waiting around in case you needed to introduce me? When you didn't know you'd be seeing me today."

"Yes." *Lina, I need some help – can you walk around from behind these trees?*

Barely a moment passed and she answered. *Just a moment and I can. You sure you want to try this?*

I am. And thanks.

Duong pulled a pair of cuffs from his pocket. "Okay, that's enough. I'm going to have to arrest you, Reed. You can tell me the rest from an interrogation room..." he trailed off.

Lina appeared from behind the tree, her Goth girl meets Iceland look complete with short black skirt, blue lipstick and pale skin, though her silvery hair was playing nice, thankfully.

"Who are you?"

"Lina, Reed's cousin." She curtseyed. "Pleased to meet you, Mr Detective Sir."

Duong turned back to Reed. "She really was here?"

"Yes, and I wanted you to meet her because she made the 'Reed' that's currently in the hospital."

Now the policeman blinked. "What?"

"I'm telling the truth, Duong."

Duong shook his head but eventually turned back to Lina. "You *made* a fake that realistic?"

"I did."

"That's impossible – it's far beyond anything I've ever seen, even those guys in Massachusetts or the robots at those Japanese hotels. They couldn't make that, *no-one* could."

She grinned. "Then what do you think happened?"

Duong jammed the cuffs back into his pocket. "I don't

know, but some Halloween-robotics-engineer scam artist didn't make a bloody android, that's for sure."

"Then what are you going to do?" Reed asked.

"Just give me a minute, all right?" he snapped, and this time he lit two cigarettes at once. "Just, both of you stay right here while I think."

"Twelve thousand, seven hundred and thirteen more cigarettes will kill you, you know," Lina told him.

Reed glared at her, but Duong had waved the comment away as he paced back and forth.

Reed, this might not be enough, you know.

He nodded slowly. *He kind of surprised me. I'm just making this up as I go, so I'd love any ideas if you've got anything?*

I do, actually. Lina leant against the bark. *Let's call Mnemosyne.*

Wiping his memory is definitely *one of the things I'm not supposed to do, and I think you know that. I'm trying* not *to draw attention, remember?*

We'll figure out a way to do that. Maybe Potter's robe, maybe I'll tell Mother that one of the Little Ones was seen, by accident. She'll be fine with that.

Reed looked back at the detective, who was sucking down his nicotine sticks as he paced. It was almost impressive – he'd had nearly half a dozen in a really short space of time. But it wouldn't be long before he'd begin arresting everyone or visiting the hospital.

We better do something, I guess. Call her, Lina.

Chapter 15.

"All right," Duong said as he ground yet another cigarette into the grass. "You're both coming with me to the hospital; we'll sort it out there."

Reed nodded. "If that's what you think is best."

"Are we taking two cars?" Lina asked.

"No," Duong barked as he started along the wide path.

"You seem grumpy."

He glared at her. "That's because I am, young lady."

"Well, now." Lina winked at him. "I do like compliments."

The detective stopped. "If you can see that I'm not in a good mood, you can give that a rest, can't you?"

She sighed. "Yes, sir."

Reed shot her a glare of his own, but by the time they reached his car – which he would have to make sure was locked up – it seemed that one of Mnemosyne's grandchildren was already waiting.

A slender man dressed in a white tunic, he wore a quill tucked into generous curls. *Anton, if I'm remembering correctly.*

"And who are you?" Duong asked.

Anton offered a smile. "I'm here to help."

"Who?" Duong turned to Reed with a glare. "Is this meant to be another one of your fancy-dress cousins or something?"

Lina skipped behind Duong and placed her hands over his eyes, almost too fast to track – and it would have been, for a regular human.

Duong collapsed into her arms, breathing deeply.

She lifted the man as though he weighed no more than a bag of chips, and motioned for Reed to get the car door. "Across back seat is best, I think. How does that suit you, Anton?"

"Perfect."

Once Lina had arranged Duong across the seats, Reed closed the door and strode around to driver's side, hopping in to find Lina was already beside him. Anton sat with Duong in the back, the detective's legs half-visible through pristine white tunic.

"So, how long for and how far back?" Anton asked. "Or, should I aim more specifically for something?"

"A year," Reed said.

"That long?" Lina asked.

"I need time to figure something out. And if we get stuck down there again, I might need it."

"Ah."

"Does that change things between you and Anton?"

Mnemosyne's grandson shook his curls. "Not at all, happy to help you both."

"Then a year, please," Reed said. "And I need him to forget that any of this happened here at the cemetery, any mention of Lina or you of course, and my double being 'created' too."

"Certainly. Anything else?"

"One more thing, if you don't mind – I want him to believe that the transfer to the psych hospital went smoothly, for him to have no desire to follow up on it," he said. "Actually, we might need someone else to have similar work done."

"I can manage that – Lina?"

She nodded. "Two pomegranates."

"Excellent."

Not the usual pomegranate, Lina was dealing in some rare fruit indeed. "Is that all too difficult?" Reed asked.

"Just like brain surgery," Anton said with a shrug.

"That easy, huh?"

"For me, yes," the man replied. "But it's not foolproof. For instance, if Duong were to see you beside your doll, or even out and about in the city, he'd suffer quite the shock."

"What kind of shock?"

"Migraines, fainting, vertigo, things like that. And he'd *definitely* know something was not right."

"When it's time, I'll ease him into it," Reed said.

"That's kind of you, Reed Lavender."

The man pulled the quill free and began writing upon Duong's forehead, though the trails of blue, green and yellow did not leave a mark.

And it did not take long before he stopped with a smile. "All done, and any time is fine for the delivery, Lina."

"As soon as I can."

Anton blinked out of sight and Reed looked to his cousin. "Can you manage that?"

"I can – they're difficult but not impossible to come by."

"Thank you, then." Reed backed from the park and started out of the cemetery, eventually joining lines of traffic heading west.

When Reed reached Duong's townhouse with its small stone garden, he parked in the driveway and sighed.

"Think this will all be enough?" Lina asked.

"I don't know. I just need some space, I think. Once we deal with Enki, we can come back and fix Duong."

"He'll still have questions, you know."

"I do," Reed said. "What about the doll?"

"Doing fine – they've been medicating it, and I'm collecting the pills and IV."

"Wait? Why?"

She shrugged. "We trade them."

"What?"

"I thought you knew. It's like when you humans and trade cards. Or those figurines people go crazy over, the movie tie-ins for supermarkets and what not."

This is new to me. "No-one's ever mentioned this before, you know."

"I admit, we might be a little ashamed."

"So, what's most rare?" Reed asked with a chuckle, then stopped. "Actually, that's not important. What about blood tests and the like? With the doll," he added.

Lina patted his cheek. "All's well in hand," she said. "It's a perfect thing you know, I just use the DNA to create whatever they try to test."

"You do?"

"Sure, it's fun!"

Reed shook his head. *So, she can basically clone me? That's something else I didn't know. This is turning into quite an educational day.* "Well, thanks, I guess."

"You're welcome. Now, let's drop him off in his bed and get back to work."

Chapter 16.

"Are you sure you can placate her, if we're caught?" Reed asked as he paced his apartment, once again shrouded in Potter's robe. So far, it was working pretty perfectly, since Aunty had not come to tear him away and send him back to the Sands.

"For ourselves? Yes," Max said. "Lina and I are favourites, you know. But I'm not so confident when it comes to you."

Lina kicked her legs from where she lay half slung across his couch, just amusing herself it seemed. "Assuming Potter's robe works... which it just might. It actually feels like he's here when you wear it, you know. We might not have to deal with that problem."

Good to know. "What about the Sands? Does she ever check on them?"

"Only if something is amiss – you know what it's like, no news is good news, after all."

"Then let's go back to Parginos," Reed said. "Mum is still down there somewhere. And Patrick too."

Lina pointed at Reed. "Slow down, cowboy. Do we

even have an idea of what to do?"

"Emma is on her way; she's been researching."

"Excellent, so have we," Max replied. "And this won't be a surprise, but Enki probably existed in the multi-state, like all the older Gods, when he was active. So, many cultures have many names for him but Lord of Water and God of Creation are two that clearly compliment Feronia."

"Makes sense."

"Exactly. But it's the 'Mischief' moniker that might give us trouble when it comes to his city."

"You think Parginos is a trick?"

"Well, not precisely. It's serious, detailed and close to complete, I think we can agree. All in all, a fair test run for when he can supplant Melbourne and beyond."

Reed almost shook his head. *Supplant Melbourne. And beyond.* Hard to actually imagine the magnitude of what that meant. For one, in the city alone it was five million people suddenly gone. *This is so far beyond my pay grade.* Yet, sitting back and doing nothing was not the answer. "But?"

"Well, we know he's aware of us, of our goal. And he knows the other Gods are sending their agents too, right?"

"Right."

"And so I worry that he'd have planned for us. It's hard to trick a trickster and Enki might be a few steps ahead of us, no matter how well we thought things went last time."

"Agree," Lina said from the couch.

Another troubling thought. "Meaning... that we should call on Laverna for advice? Even among trickster Gods I don't think we should trust her."

"Actually, I was thinking of something else," Max replied. "Someone who bested our Radiant King long ago, someone he would have known quite well." He paused, gesturing to Reed, as if expecting an answer.

"Ancient Sumerian Gods aren't exactly my specialty."

"Very well. It's 'Ninhursag', I was looking for 'Ninhursag', Reed. A Mother Goddess, you know," he said with a sigh. "Lose four hundred dollars, by the way."

Ninhursag? Hadn't Emma placed that name on her own list? "Emma was researching Ninhursag too. Why her?"

Lina sat up. "We need to find her because she was able to 'outsmart' him before, and she's not a trickster herself. Whatever she can tell us will actually be useful."

"We hope," Max added.

Reed nodded. "Let's do it, how do we find her? Is she a Fragment or a Stray God? Something more like Enki?"

"Probably a Stray," Lina replied.

"That's something, at least," Reed said. Chasing Fragments was nearly impossible. *Far beyond my meagre gifts.* "Any ideas?"

Max clapped his hands together. "Off to Mesopotamia!"

"Join us in the twenty-first century, can you?"

"Sorry."

"And that's a big region to search, you know. I can't afford to fly to Iraq or Kuwait – or anywhere nearby either, for that matter."

"Not to worry, I was thinking of something a little different," Max said. "Normally yes, we'd seek old holy places or texts and sometimes descendant worshippers to help tether a Stray, but I think that's not the fastest choice available."

"What's quicker?"

"Down the rabbit hole of memory. We'll find a way in through the dead, and collect traces of Ninhursag that way so we can perform a summoning."

"Is that possible?"

"Of course," he said. "But it's not done very often. Mother disapproves, generally – the dead ought not be disturbed unless it's time for the wheel, but she'll make an exception."

"You're fond of saying that."

"Yes, but I mean it. She commanded us to get the job done and this is what we need to do."

"Can I even help? It doesn't sound like the Fringe."

"Potter's robe and scythe should be enough, especially considering your Reaper heritage."

"Just don't take it off," Lina added.

"What if something goes wrong?"

"We'd have to get used to the memories of long-dead Mesopotamians, I suppose," she said.

"All of us?"

"Well, memories can be pretty powerful, especially shared ones that have lasted so long," she said. "Mother could probably retrieve us if needed... I think. Maybe."

"Wait, are you saying even Mors couldn't free us?"

"A better way to describe it might be that I don't want to find out she *can't*, so I'll be taking precautions."

Max nodded. "And yours are already in place, so just bring that robe and scythe."

"Deal," Reed said, tension nevertheless growing in his limbs. "When do we begin?"

"Tomorrow should give us enough time to locate a few likely souls, I'd say – until then, sleep well."

Max disappeared.

Lina waved from the couch, as she too blinked out of sight, and then he was alone.

Chapter 17.

Thumping upon Reed's front door woke him.

He groaned but still rolled from bed. Once upright, he skirted the hastily-patched hole in the floor that the Radiant King had left, and stumbled into pants with a sigh. The apartment already stuffy from summer heat outside. Sweat coated his bare chest and when he ran a hand through the hair on his head, it was damp.

Another knock came from the door. *It's probably Emma.* She'd been held up last night but had promised to bring what she'd found in the morning, and now he'd kept her waiting by sleeping late.

Reed opened the door. "Emma, I–"

Grace stood in the doorway, bare arms folded, pale hair tied into a topknot. "You're actually home for once."

"Grace?"

"Where's Patrick, Reed? Devin and I have been looking for *weeks*."

He opened his door wider. "Come in."

She strode into the room, not glancing around. Her jaw

was clenched and the muscles in her arms were just as tense. "Well?"

"In a place called Parginos – something took him." *And he better be alive, not just for my sake.* Grace looked like she was restraining her anger with some effort. New as Patrick was, if he'd already been accepted into the pack then she and Devin would protect him, that simple. *And they already are.*

"What thing?"

"A puppet created by a Sumerian God. It's serious, Grace, and I'm sorry I haven't told you yet–"

She leapt across the room. A clawed hand caught him by the throat, lifting him from his feet. A silvery wolf stood before him, muscles rippling beneath fur. He caught her arm for balance, legs dangling, but did not fight. "I've been trapped myself," he managed.

"You should have found a way to send word!"

"Sorry, I was distracted."

"What?" She shook him, and he bit the inside of his check. Warm blood filled his mouth.

"The puppet was made from pieces of my father."

The anger in her bright eyes faded. "Your father?"

"Yes."

Grace lowered him, shifting back to her human form, white singlet and jeans instead of fur. "What does that even mean?"

Reed rubbed at his throat. "Let me get some water. Want something?"

She shook her head as she followed him to the kitchen.

At the tap, Reed paused to fill a glass. *Dad, are you really gone now?* "Enki abducted my parents, years ago. That's why they disappeared. It can't remember if I've ever told you or Devin?"

"You mentioned it."

"Well, all this time Enki has been using them to make a city beneath Melbourne – and the puppet he sent up here was made from the skin, and flesh and bones of my Father. He told me himself," Reed said. "Mum's still down there somewhere, and so is Patrick. I followed, but I didn't find him. We're going back though, once we have a way to stop Enki."

She was silent a moment. "Reed, I'm sorry. Will you let me help?"

"Of course," he said with a small smile. "I'm not sure when we'll be ready to go back down there, but Max and Lina have a plan, something we have to do first. We've only got a month or two though."

"Then what should me and Devin do?"

Reed glanced down into the sink, where a sponge sat like a pink raft on a seamless silver ocean. "While I'm away, you might need to get someone to look after the gym – time isn't the same down there."

"We will. But what about *now*, Reed? I'm not just going to sit around."

"I don't know."

She put a hand on her hip. "What about some hunting up here?"

Reed paused, glass half-raised. "Actually, maybe you could. Would Devin and the others help?"

"What are we hunting?"

"Well, maybe *seeking* is a better word – I don't want you to take too many risks."

"Everything is going to be a risk if we want to get Patrick back."

He sighed. "Right. Well, it's Enki, the Radiant King. I want to know if he's sent any more puppets up here. If you can get a scent, will that be enough?"

"Excellent – I'll get started right now," she said, heading for the door.

"Thanks." Reed turned back to the kitchen and started on breakfast, just toast and butter – real butter, not margarine – and he'd barely taken two bites before Emma arrived.

"Reed, your front door is open."

"I know. It's fine." He offered Emma a drink and then gave her an update on Max and Lina's plan, adding the visit from Grace too. "How did you go with the song?"

She grinned. "I have it settled now, there *is* a link and so it's probably a variant of the ancient melody so I think we can use it. Even without bells, most of us could probably hum it at least."

"That's something."

"Well, I'm going to collect some bells or maybe a lyre and get practising," she said as she stood. Her cheer had faded a little. "Are you sure about going with Max and Lina?"

"I think it will work."

Emma gave him a nudge in his chair. "No, I mean is it safe?"

"So long as I keep masquerading as Potter." He stood and pulled her into his arms. "You sound worried."

"I am."

He hesitated before speaking; the words could have

gone unsaid but he wanted to say them. "This is getting serious again, isn't it?"

"Yeah, but you knew that, you big idiot."

He smiled. "Yeah. You be careful too."

She gave him a squeeze. "I will."

***

Max and Lina took him into the Fringe the very moment they arrived, but he did not step into a grey, listless and overheated version of his apartment as would have been customary. Instead, Reed stood within a darkened room lit by a single column of light – light that somehow glittered where it fell upon a sun-dial.

The stone was old, grey, almost blue, with a face of polished silver. The points did not have recognisable symbols, but the dial itself stood like the sail of a boat. It sparkled beneath the shimmering light.

"Where are we?" Reed asked into the quiet.

"A terminus," Lina said. "We can reach the various memories from here – we might have to chase a few, however."

"You mean, by actually running?"

"No, not so much with your legs."

"Then do you mean –"

Max waved a hand. "When the time comes, I'll explain. For now, we've got a steep climb ahead." He reached out to touch a symbol and the dial started to turn, almost billowing as it did. "Not that Lina and I need any of this; these trappings are more a physical representation for the benefit of your mind. You see, what's really happening is–"

"Thank you, Max but I don't think I can handle the metaphysics."

"A shame. I always thought I'd thrive in the academic community."

"Max."

"Fine, fine."

The dial stopped upon one of the symbols. Darkness resolved into a wind-swept mountainside, pale stone and dust, the dark pines clinging to the sides of a winding trail. Cuneiform Markers of stone offered some information, but he couldn't read it.

Storm-clouds broiled overhead but no rain or thunder came... yet?

"Enough gawking, Reed," Max called from ahead.

Reed climbed after them, the trail steep but not unbearable, especially with the robe shielding him from the elements. He kept Potter's scythe ready but no immediate threats appeared. *And it did seem like the danger was going to be from being trapped here.*

"What are we looking for here?"

"The site of a miracle, as her worshippers probably termed it," Max replied. "Shouldn't be too hard to find, once we reach the fork."

And Max was right, not long after the path forked, they reached a plateau where a stone shrine overlooked a valley of trees, a stretching plain of white and grey rock beyond.

There, his cousin examined the carving of Ninhursag with her halo, and then he nodded.

"Did that help?" Reed asked.

"It did. Let's try another memory," Max said, leading them back down the mountain – only this time it was only a few steps before the silver sundial appeared, bringing its pool of light and its darkness.

Lina touched a symbol this time, and once again the sail shifted. "This one might be a little more interactive, it's hard to know."

But when the sail stopped there was only a new darkness where a beautiful but stern-looking woman waited. She wore a long dress or robe of green and blue with diagonal divisions to its... sections? The proper description escaped him, or maybe he just didn't know enough about Ancient Mesopotamian clothing for his mind to recognise what he saw?

Her long dark hair was held back by a headband – he recognised that much, and though she had no halo now, there *was* a lion cub at her bare feet.

"Young one." Her voice rang out and with it came the force of her – a Goddess, yet he was not driven to his knees, *she* was lessened. Even her form flickered.

Ninhursag.

"You seek me because Enki stirs. I stir because *he* seeks to return."

Reed knelt. Would the gesture appease her? "We do, My Lady. We want to ask for your help. Can he be stopped?"

"Certainly, as we all might fade and return and fade again." A pause. "You must feed him exactly what he seeks, for he will find it far too painful."

"Does he seek... me?"

"No, your family was a means to an end. What Enki seeks is simple enough – knowledge, as always. The knowledge to create, to reap, destroy and restore. Yet in his slow awakening, he has forgotten a bitter truth. That truth will be enough for me aid you. I will strike when he is weakened."

"Strike?"

"Yes."

"Thank you, My Lady. But how do we use knowledge..." Reed trailed off.

She was gone and once again, he found himself standing before the silver dial with Max and Lina. "You heard that?" he asked. The sense of Ninhursag lingered, a lurking determination.

"We did," Max replied.

"This went better than I was expecting," Lina added. "And Ninhursag seemed nice, don't you think?"

"Let's continue this somewhere else, can we?" Reed asked. "And maybe focus on her advice first?"

Lina rolled her eyes. "Work, work, work, huh?"

"Exactly, and you can keep insulting me then too, but we have a deadline, you know."

She stuck her tongue out and then the dial and the darkness disappeared.

Chapter 18.

"How do you feed a god too much knowledge?" Reed asked as he undid a few buttons at the top of his shirt, offering a slight frown at the hothouse and its wealth of greenery; pinks and blues mixed in. *It is nice to meet somewhere else for a change, I suppose.* "And what 'bitter truth' has he forgotten?"

"A worthy question," Max said from behind the silver bar, where he was sprinkling herbs and spices over frying chicken. Paprika, basil and rosemary? "We could seek her again, I suppose. But it might not bear fruit – she obviously chooses when and whether to speak to those who seek her."

"At least it sounds like she finds us useful," Lina added.

Everyone was gathered together again, as they had before the first assault on Parginos. Only now, Max and Lina hosted a few extra faces; it wasn't just Emma and Diego who were along for the ride this time. Both Grace and Devin joined them for the meal, along with Adrina. And while she appeared her usual impassive self, with her brown tunic, bare feet and longbow nearby, the werewolves were just a touch wide-eyed.

"I'm still interested in whether we can combine Emma's

song with this new possibility," Lina said. "It's a little familiar."

"If I may?" Diego asked, waiting for nods. "What if there is another approach available? We focus much of our energy on Enki, firstly, and that is a prudent choice but is it our *only* option?"

"You're thinking of Feronia?" Emma asked.

He rested his giant forearms upon the table. "Perhaps. If Enki was strong enough, or 'present' enough to create his city by himself, I believe he would have done so. Instead, he has required Feronia's help."

Reed nodded. "We put a stop to her and we cut off the power he needs."

"He'll know she's a target," Max said, but he sounded excited. "We have to be ready. More so than our last soiree."

"If I can find my parents then maybe they'll know something we can use."

"Should we split into two groups, then?" Diego suggested.

"Let's eat first – and tell me if I'm getting any better as a chef," Max said as he carried a small mountain of steaming chicken to the table, more than enough for the human and mostly-human present, but there was no side dish. "Thought I'd focus on one element this time."

Reed had to chuckle, but he speared a few slabs with his fork and added them to his plate. *It certainly smells good.* The werewolves were already eating, and Emma seemed pleased enough. His first bite confirmed that yes, Max was getting better. And when he informed his cousin of the fact, a beaming smile was a nice reward.

"Speaking of hunting, how did your search go?" Max asked Grace and Devin once they'd finished their meal.

"We did find something at St Kilda beach. But the trail disappeared east of the city," Grace said. "It had the same scent but it seemed smaller, somehow."

"Like, fainter?" Reed asked.

"Not really. I got the impression that whatever had bored up through the sandy earth was not as big as the thing that visited you."

Devin nodded. "We've sent a few of the boys out to cast a wider net but so far nothing."

"I can call some hunters to aid you," Adrina offered.

"That'd be great."

Reed was frowning at his now empty plate. Another runaway? If something serious was on the loose again, then the whole cycle might end up repeating once Enki was dealt with. *Make that* if *we can deal with him.*

"How do we stop Feronia's hand then?" Emma asked.

"Leave that to me." Lina flickered out of sight, and then returned with a head-sized beaker of white powder. It was actually not unlike a fishbowl with a long neck at the top. "This is pure Cantarella; we'll mix it with some herbicide."

Reed leant a little closer. "The famous poison favoured by the Borgia family? It's actually real?"

"Most people think it was just arsenic," she said. "But I know Mars and Laverna have lent it out on occasion, so humans have used it in the past, yes."

"And this will work?" Adrina asked.

"I believe so."

She frowned.

"Problem, dear cousin?" Max asked.

"It hardly seems an honourable way to hunt an enemy."

"But use it we must."

Reed stood. "This could work. Let's finish whatever other precautions we need to take and head back down there – I'll pick up some herbicide while Emma teaches you the song. Agreed?"

"Yes, sir!" Max said, snapping his heels together and giving a salute.

***

Returning to Parginos was easier than Reed had suspected. This time Max and Lina took them directly back into the city itself, bypassing the inverted tower and its odd doorman.

"We're actually using the same path," Max explained. "But I've simplified it, a little like the folding of space done by the Fringe."

"And Enki is just letting you do this?" Reed asked.

"It seems so – which is troubling, of course."

As before, though it was a pleasant 'day' overhead, no-one was out and about enjoying the fine weather in the streets. And while Devin and Grace looked around at the slightly 'off' shops and signs with narrowed eyes, Adrina seemed unperturbed. She *did* walk with an arrow nocked, but nothing about her expression or cool stride suggested worry.

No-one spoke much at all, but Reed kept close to Emma and her golden lyre. He had the Sonorous, and Devin, Grace and Diego carried other bells – common bells, but together they'd be able to form the sequence of notes, if needed.

Perhaps more importantly, at least first, was the barrel of Cantarella and weed-killer that the Minotaur carried over one shoulder. His other shoulder bore more water from Dionysus' fountain and Emma had already painted symbols on the others.

We're as ready as we can be. And this time, I have Potter's robe and scythe. This time would be different, surely. *Just finish off Feronia, draw out Enki and then send him off with the song. Or at least, weaken him enough for Ninhursag to strike.*

Or would the supposed bitter truth still need to be shared?

Without knowing what that truth was, however, such a plan seemed like a long shot.

When they finally reached the park with its mismatched flora and fauna, Reed found that the mound of pale skulls at the Fountain of Leaves had not changed. Twin rib bones still suggested a pear or even a teardrop, and water still flowed across the bones like a film of glittering skin.

"I can't feel Enki at all. Feronia's not very strong here either," Max said when they stopped.

So, one thing has changed after all.

The sense of searing sand *was* gone, replaced by the purple scent of decay.

"Maybe he has truly abandoned this place?" Emma said.

"Or it's all part of a trap," Adrina added.

"Let's hurry then." Reed lifted the scythe and waited for Diego to place the cask of poison onto the rune-covered pile of skulls and step back.

Reed then glanced around at the others. "We don't really know what'll happen, so be ready." He tried not to let his gaze linger on Emma, tried not to let his concern accidently unnerve *her*, but she only smiled back, lyre in hand.

Max and Lina nodded, one hand each interlocked around a transparent staff they produced from... somewhere. *I have to assume it's useful for dealing with Feronia somehow.* Adrina herself stood ready, bow in hand.

"Will this really work?" Grace asked, glancing around the park. Her claws were out, same as Devin.

"We have to find out." Reed swung Potter's scythe.

Light flashed like a scalpel, slicing the container open. The top half fell free and pale *Cantarella* and herbicide spilled across the bones. Steam followed, the hissing scent of something sweet hitting him like a smack to the face.

Reed fell back, eyes stinging.

Shit, did I just poison myself?

From somewhere deep below, a high-pitched wail rose. Even muffled by the earth, the note was so shrill that Reed dropped the scythe to clamp both hands over his ears. Max and Lina were chanting, staff raised, one hand each holding it, but the scream continued.

Reed fell to the ground with a curse now. The pitch increased and so did the pain with it – like a migraine being forced in through his ears. *Gods be damned, how much worse is this going to get?* He pulled the hood right over his face and the fabric helped a little. *How bad must this be for the wolves? And Emma?*

Something wrapped around his ankle.

It jerked him across the ground.

"Reed!" Emma's shout filled the sudden vacuum left as the piercing shriek disappeared.

A mottled green tendril was dragging him back toward the mound and its wreaths of pungent steam. Reed fumbled for the scythe, fingers grasping it. He swung, a jolt of panic skewing his aim, but the slice cut enough that the tendril immediately shrivelled to black and then grey ash, fluttering away.

Free.

Reed lifted himself up, breathing hard as he glanced to where Max and Lina held a now faintly-glowing staff, the touch of green very pale. "Is it done?"

"Yes. Feronia is now little more than a Stray, trapped in this staff," Lina said, a trace of sadness in her voice.

"And what about Enki?" Emma asked as she looked to Reed, concern in her gaze.

"Indeed," Max replied.

Chapter 19.

The Radiant King had abandoned Parginos.

Or so it seemed.

Without any manner of proof, Reed wasn't ready to rule out some other ploy. *No assumptions.* Yet when he sat within the warm interior of Raelene's chicken shop once more, his mother's voice drifting down from the speakers, it was impossible to deny that *something* about the city had changed.

It no longer held a general watchfulness, a feeling he hadn't fully appreciated last visit. But now that the feeling was gone, or at least far, far duller, he did. *Which doesn't really make sense.*

While Raelene worked on their drinks, Max lowered his voice. "This place might be a bigger problem than I thought."

"How so?" Reed asked.

"Well, what did you want to do with these people?"

"What do you mean?"

He sighed. "They aren't precisely human – at least, not

in the way that Emma is, nor your lesser half. And they seem to have a shorter lifespan in exchange for the regular cycling."

"Spell it out for me," Reed said. "And 'lesser'? Nice one, cousin."

"You know what I mean."

Lina took over. "He's trying to say that if these twenty or so Parginos people join Melbourne's population, then medically their bodies and lifespan will draw unwanted attention, and that's just the ones who look quite human. It could be a horrible life if these people are captured and dissected and studied, or if they basically end up being alone for an eternity."

Max was nodding. "And something equally troubling could happen. If they breed with regular humans, they might create a generation of people with doomed or repeating cycles."

"Oh." Reed sighed. *That* is *a concern but perhaps it's one for the future. Enki has to be stopped before we can help them.* "I see your point, but shouldn't we deal with Enki first? And once again, your vocab is a little on the insulting side."

"Sorry, again. I know 'regular' can be a bit of a negative but if you think about it, being normal has advantages–"

"I meant 'breed', just so you're aware."

Raelene appeared with their drinks, setting them down with her rosy smile. "I must admit, I was surprised to see you again, and bringing some lovely new faces too."

"It's nice to be back," Reed said.

"Well, your timing is perfect. You just missed a commotion over at the Fountain."

"First Day trouble?" Lina asked.

The owner fussed with the tray. "Well, Kiri couldn't really say but she was going to ask Lucas, since he's been so edgy of late."

"Can we help at all?"

"I'm not sure, dear. But don't worry yourself, over it," she said, started back for the kitchen.

Reed half rose. "Raelene, just one more question?"

"Of course."

"If we do see something unusual, should we report it to Kiri? I'm not sure where the Watch is located, is all."

"Oh, it's not all that far," she said, giving directions.

"Thank you so much," Reed said, then proceeded to rush everyone through their drinks, not that anyone protested, and then it was back into the streets. There, they headed west to cut through an empty petrol station with its blue and black stripes, to reach another thoroughfare and the home of the Watch.

It was not a subtle building.

Weapons, weapons and more weapons lay behind barred windows, from knives to guns, grenades and even coloured vials. They might have all been real too but Reed couldn't be sure. Even with the arsenal, it was actually a huge slogan in yellow resting above the door that caught his eye. It urged the residents to 'Accept' and then in smaller lettering beneath, 'First Day Changes'.

"Full marks for clear messaging," Reed said before opening the door.

Within, the weapons were absent, or at least, confined to the front window. The decoration he found was more warm wood-tones with curved furniture and pastoral paintings. Not unlike a hunting lodge, only the paintings were not of animals he recognised and the forests were coloured of pinks and purples.

The scene of lavender lingered too – an equally dissonant touch.

Two figures spoke at a large desk, one was Kiri in her long yellow coat, dark curls blocking the view of her conversation partner. But as Reed led everyone closer, he came to recognise the fellow in the Akubra and blue suit, his sunken eyes giving him something of a sullen expression. *A change from his whistling on our first visit.*

"Oh, you've returned?" Kiri said, but her surprise quickly shifted to concern as she rose. "I have to warn you all, please stay away from the Fountain of Leaves. Something is wrong there."

"Is it truly?" the man asked.

She glanced back at him, and though it seemed by her narrowed eyes that she was frustrated with him, she did not raise her voice. "You know it's better to accept, Lucas. The First Day comes to us all."

He shook his head but did not reply.

"Actually, you may not be able to be reborn from the Fountain any longer," Reed said.

Kiri folded her arms now. "Why?"

"Because the power behind that mound of skulls is no longer there," Max explained, his own voice gentle. "It was a somewhat mindless Goddess, but she is no longer being manipulated by the one who built this place: Enki."

"Wait..." Kiri's brown eyes widened. "No, what are you talking about? You know of Enki? How could he let this happen?"

Lina glanced to Max. "It almost sounds like you can

communicate with him, Kiri."

"All in the Watch can," she said. "As always. But I can't believe what you're saying."

"I'm afraid it's true," Reed replied. "But we need to know where he went, if he truly left this place. And it might not be safe for you here anymore."

"Why?"

Lucas had straightened too.

"Enki might not have been fully honest with the people of Parginos," he said, choosing his words with some care. Just dumping the truth would not win them any allies.

"What does that mean, stranger?" Lucas asked.

"Enki does not lie to his people," Kiri said.

"He has already taken people from above. Our friend Patrick among... others," he said after a slight pause. Kiri's arms were still folded and so claiming that 'Capri' was actually his mother didn't seem useful either. "That's why we've returned."

"I cannot believe any of this," Kiri said. "You all wait here."

And then she charged out into the street, leaving Reed and the others alone with Lucas, whose eyes bore a hopeful glint.

"Who are you people?" he asked.

Adrina spun. "I think she's changed her mind."

Kiri's yellow coat reappeared outside, and she clapped her hands together with a shout. A wave swept through the weapons and glass, distorting their proportions and colours, and bringing a smothering shadow with it.

Chapter 20.

When the darkness fluttered away, like leaves caught in wind, it revealed a ghoulish, open maw *very* similar to what could be found at Luna Park's entry. The famous 'Mr Moon' face, a perfect source of nightmare fuel that now towered over him.

The real thing was a cross between a seedy harlequin and the moon, with spiked rays from the sun behind it – but this one bore serpentine eyes and teeth dripping with a sparkling slime. Obviously, the entrance to the St Kilda theme park was the inspiration for Enki, but what confronted Reed was not something which had been refurbished who knew how many times since 1912, not at all. The opening before him was not Melbourne itself.

This is certainly even less welcoming.

Kiri had not sent him *from* Parginos at all.

Reed turned, only to find three more faces, mouths gaping – each at least three stories tall, and revealing other squares of light. He lifted his voice. "Emma? Max?"

Only echoes answered. Reed lifted Potter's scythe and

started forward, avoiding the dripping substance as he crossed into the mouth's shadow. *It probably won't be a problem for the robe, but who knows?*

And in the next patch of light, another four openings, each a Mr Moon face.

He continued in a straight line.

The same result.

"Fine." Reed turned left, then walked straight beneath the next set of giant teeth. Over and over he chose directions at random, seeking any hint of difference but found none. Once again, he shouted into the endless rooms and waited for a response.

In the quiet that followed, Reed leant against one of the walls. Solid stuff – it wasn't a constructed space, the skylight above was truly letting light in; it was just too high to reach, even if he climbed one of the distorted Mr Moon faces.

Which left the Fringe... yet he hesitated.

If he could reach the Fringe – with or without the scythe – and escape, doing so meant leaving the others behind, at least until he could return with help. *Patrick is still down here somewhere, along with Mum. I can't let Emma and the others get added to that list.*

He walked on, once again choosing directions at random, seeking any variation.

And finally, he found it.

A woman stood within a patch of light – not Emma and not Grace.

Delicate, almost elfin features, dark hair, and standing in a long blue skirt and dark jacket. She was somewhat transparent.

And *very* familiar.

Very.

"Mum?"

She waved him closer.

Reed charged through the tunnel to skid to a stop before her. *It is her!* Like he remembered from all those years ago – right down to the same clothes. Nothing had changed, she hadn't aged either. *Just like Dad.* But unlike when Reed met his father, when he tried to embrace his mother, his arms found nothing.

But she smiled at him, and spoke, her voice distant. "Are you getting enough sleep, honey?"

He blinked back the sting of tears. "Not really."

"I guess I'll have to worry about that later. Let's get out of here, first."

"How?" A *million* other questions could have echoed in the strange maze, but that one was first out the door. "Where are you?"

"There's a broadcast tower. Just follow Wintergreen Avenue east."

"You're trapped in there?"

She sighed. "Well, in a way. It's a mouthful of a story."

"What about Enki?"

"He's gone. Something's happening but I can't find him, and I've been looking."

"Then he's abandoned the city?"

"Maybe." She began to fade. "Hurry, Reed, and don't worry about your friends. They're safe for now."

"Where...?"

She was gone. He turned, but the walls were still in place, nothing had changed about his prison. Wherever she was, whatever Enki had done, it was still blocking her power as a Reaper.

Reed lifted Potter's scythe. "Time to get creative."

He swung at the nearest wall of black.

The blade sliced through effortlessly, light and colour pouring inside. Beyond, the mostly realistic streets of Parginos were revealed, complete with their minor imperfections. Reed swung again and tore his way free from the maze, bursting onto the pavement. Again, as with so many other parts of the city, it was empty of human life.

If not for a faint breeze and the shuffling leaves back and forth between gutters, there would have been no movement at all.

East on Wintergreen Avenue.

Reed ran up the centre of the street, passing letter boxes and parked cars from half a dozen eras, heading for glimpses of a huge white broadcast tower between buildings.

When he reached it he stumbled to a stop to catch his breath. *Shit, I'm not in good shape at all.*

The tower reared up from a small park like a pale spearhead, ringed by purple and green willow trees, their tresses waving in a rising wind. Lights blinked from several of the dishes but there was still no real sense of any people nearby.

Not Enki.

Nor Mum either.

But a brick and weatherboard building did lurk at the foot of the tower, obscured by the tree trunks.

Reed jogged along the path and came to a wire fence, its gate locked. Before him, leaves littered the roof, where a single, plump kookaburra sat. It rested above a sign that said only 'Capri'.

Potter's scythe flashed.

Reed stepped over the ruined fence and strode to the door where he tried the handle – locked. Once again, he swung his weapon. The handle and lock clattered to the step and he entered a brightly-lit office. It contained desks with computer screens and calendars, coffee mugs and pens, everything exceptionally normal – despite a banner which misspelt the word 'Birthday'.

Two doors.

One led to a server room, that blinked and hummed quietly, and the other was a break room that featured adjoining toilet and basin, its door ajar. Reed nudged it open with his foot, but the room was empty.

"Just like the rest of this place."

One desk featured an active screensaver – rainbow bars, and a set of headphones. Reed sat and placed them on, and sure enough, there Capri was 'singing' one of her odd 'songs'.

"Mum?"

The song continued, but her voice also spoke to him through the music, louder, more emotive. "Reed? Can you destroy the server?"

"I have Potter's scythe."

"Perfect, honey. If you can, one part of me will be free. Enough to find the others."

"One part? What do you mean?"

"Enki has separated different aspects of me, to help give the city life, to help create and then control the people here. Before he took Feronia's hand, your father and I were all he had."

"So, if I smash this place to pieces, you can restore yourself and we can find Dad? And everyone else?" Reed asked as he rose, hands on the headphones. "He told me that together, you and I could save him."

"I hope so," she said, after what seemed like a split second of hesitation.

Footsteps thundered near from outside.

"How did you escape?" a voice demanded. Kiri stood in the doorway, her eyes wide. "What are you doing here?"

Reed set the headphones down gently. "What does Enki tell the Watch about this place?"

She narrowed her eyes. "Let me ask the questions. How did you escape the maze?"

Reed hefted the scythe. "It was like cutting through silk, Kiri – and that goes for pretty much anything here, I'd say. But please tell me, do you know the history of the one you serve? It's important."

Her gaze lingered on the weapon but she didn't make any threatening moves, no doubt wary of him. "What history?"

"Enki created this city, and he used my parents to do so. And if you want to know the truth, 'Capri' will tell you herself."

"That's a lie. All of it."

"What did he tell you about Parginos?"

"That this place grew from a desperate need, from the failures of other cities."

Reed stepped back, giving her plenty of room, positioning himself nearer the server at the same time. "What do you have to lose by listening? Do you think Capri will lie?"

Kiri glared across as him as she stalked into the room, and raised one of the headphones to an ear, keeping watch on Reed.

Yet her suspicion did not last; as she listened, her eyes widened and her free hand became a trembling fist.

Finally, she dropped the headphones. "Is it all true, then? Everything you've told me? How?"

"Yes," Reed said softly. "And we could use your help."

Kiri looked away, wiping at her eyes. "But he told me that we were created of his good will. That we'll change the world for the better."

"Then confront him with us. Ask your questions."

She slumped back into the chair. "Nothing makes sense now."

"I know how that feels," Reed said as he approached, then rested a hand on her shoulder a moment. "We'll help you, Kiri. We'll help everyone in Parginos, if you can trust us."

She looked up at him, the uncertainty and hurt still evident in her eyes. "Are you really her son?"

"Yes. And I miss her – and my father," he said. "Can you help me make things right?"

Kiri nodded.

Chapter 21.

A spectral figure rose from the jagged ruins of plastic and steel, all melted together in a heap of what was once the server. But the figure did not solidify. Instead, the voice of Capri rang in his mind, and in Kiri's mind too, judging from the way she gave a little jump.

Meet me at the Fountain of Leaves, Reed. I'll be back soon; I think I can find my sight. Be careful of the water, something's wrong.

She was already fading as Reed reached out. "Wait..."

But she was gone.

Reed turned to Kiri. "Does Enki tell you where he goes, specifically?"

She shook her head, taking a moment. Still shocked at meeting Capri? Understandable. "Nothing, no. As the Watch, I'm usually the only one who can reach him directly but the transistor at the shop has been silent for days."

"Is that unusual?"

"I usually hear something once a day at the least, morning and night."

"Does Enki ever stop communication at other times?"

She nodded. "When he invites visitors it sometimes takes a day or two."

"Could that be what this is?"

"There's no schedule. Visitors just appear and we're supposed to talk to them about the 'outside', keep them away from the Fountain and then he takes them back, like normal... but this feels different."

"Which is what you and Raelene took us for?"

"Yes," she said. "It's rare for a visitor to come to the city twice but it's happened."

"So, the visitors are all taken back?"

Kiri shrugged. "That's what Enki tells us."

Reed leant back against the wall, glancing at the broken circuits, tiny fragments of glass and steel stuck in the carpet now. "It'd be too much of a coincidence for that to be happening now. There must be another reason. Where's everyone else?"

"After I sent you all to the maze I checked the Fountain," she said with a pause and a wince. "I tried to call the master but he did not answer. And I'm not sure where your friends are now."

"But why did you come here?" Reed asked. "How did you know this is where I'd be?"

"As the Watch, I know where every Parginos citizen is..." Kiri trailed off, then shot upright. "Lucas!"

She scrambled her way out of the building, sprinting across the path and leaping over the ruined gate.

"What's happening?" Reed cried as he followed. Hadn't Lucas been the dissatisfied guy she'd been talking to before?

"Lucas is trying to get out."

"Out? How?"

"The Ladder. Come on," she said when he caught up, then took his wrist and pulled him into the centre of the road. There, the imperfections and painted lines flew by beneath his feet, as though running atop a swift escalator.

Streets and buildings flashed at the edge of his vision as they travelled not back toward the city centre, but to an edge – more space appeared between the buildings now, small gardens, empty parking lots and playing fields, soccer and hockey goals mixing on the one surface.

But when Kiri stopped, it was before a water tower of rust-coloured stone, once a rich cream-colour but now the streaks and smudges made it seem somehow diseased, the few windows narrow and covered in dirt.

A single figure stood at the base, using an axe to hack away at a cage of razor wire that barred access to a ladder.

Lucas, his suit-jacket abandoned, sweat visible on the back of his white shirt.

Beyond, the steel rungs of a ladder stretched up toward a grated walkway, but what exactly waited at the top was nothing Reed could tell from below. Obviously, by the effort Lucas was putting into his swings, it was worth striving for – an exit, according to Kiri.

"Lucas!" she called his name as she neared, still keeping out of the swing zone.

He spun. "No. I'm leaving."

"Don't do this, please."

Lucas continued to strike the barrier. "Something needs to change."

Footsteps approached, a modest rumble, and Reed found a few familiar faces in the small crowd that rushed forward with expressions of shock and concern. Raelene still in her apron, eyes wide, and the Cat-Man almost snarling; no cute basket this time. Most of the other folks were human or at least humanoid, one fellow stout like a post box but smiling brightly, and an older fellow he recognised.

Fox Robington, for whom the bronze statue had been made.

And while the fellow carried his hockey-racquet-thing and seemed solid enough, he was grey – literally. His hair and skin, his eyes, his teeth and tongue when he spoke, all varying shades of grey or white, little streaks of black left in his stubble. "Lucas, do not threaten us all."

"I threaten no-one," he cried without turning. His next blow rattled the entire cage of razor wire. "This will all continue for you lot and I will be free, that's all."

"Kiri, stop him already!" Raelene urged.

Cat-Man nodded, claws flexing.

Kiri took a step closer, and a small splash followed.

Reed blinked down at his own feet.

Water.

Clear running water, rising steadily. *Just like Mum warned.*

A wet thump rose from the ground near the water tower but the structure did not shake or tremble – it was stony earth and asphalt that seemed to be buckling. Water and air bubbled up, splashing into little fountains all around. None were too powerful but the rate of the water's rising was the real problem.

It was already at his ankles.

Murmurs rose from the Parginos citizens, questions at first, then demands and cries for help not far behind. Whether they cried out to Kiri or Lucas or the Radiant

King, all voices soon began to blend into noise. One fellow turned to sprint back toward the city proper, perhaps seeking high ground, but the others were looking to the tower as they pleaded.

But Enki did not answer and Kiri had folded her arms, eyes closed as her mouth moved, forming silent words.

The water rose faster, surging from the very earth and street in spouts – the level now at Reed's shin. *This is getting out of hand.*

Kiri flung her arm forth and the wall of razor wire flew aside, freeing a path to the ladder. "This is a test!" she shouted. "We can wait it out, just climb the tower."

Lucas was already six feet up.

"That can't be what this is," one of the women in the crowd replied, her needle-like features in a scowl. "It's a punishment."

"No, it's temptation," someone else cried. "Lucas is doomed!"

"Enki wouldn't do that!"

"But the water isn't stopping."

Someone pushed from the back. "Let me through."

The wide-eyed man charged after Lucas, water spraying with every step, leaping for the lower rungs.

For just a moment there was a hush, a catching of breath where the smack of boots on the ladder seemed to ring out across the entire city, and then the crowd broke for the tower, shoving and trampling.

Someone knocked Fox Robington down and two others fell as the small mob charged. Kiri went for Fox and Reed started forward too. Before the crowd even reached the base of the water tower, they were fighting over who should climb first.

One of the few children, a boy of maybe ten, splashed down when a woman kicked him aside.

Cat-Man slashed with his claws, bright blood from deep scratches flying.

And he won free too, climbing swiftly.

Reed ran to the boy, kneeling in the water and lifting the dazed lad. "Are you all right?"

The boy nodded, blinking golden eyes. *I think so.*

"Good." Reed answered in reflex, then paused. "Wait, you have telepathy?"

What's happening?

"I don't know," Reed said as he lifted the boy in one arm and stepped back, giving the crowd room. Two people were struggling to clamber over the stout fellow – using him as a stepping stone.

"Stop this!" Kiri cried from where she was helping Fox to his feet. He seemed unsteady but was alive.

But no-one heeded her advice.

She can stop them, but some might die. She's hesitating. The boy's voice was sad in Reed's mind.

So, you have chosen. A new voice boomed – it too ringing from within his head.

Reed flinched.

The Radiant King stood beside the tower, half its height, blazing eyes in a shadowed face. His torso was bare but only rags covered his waist, shimmering with silver thread. The blackened Helios remained, though it seemed made of smoke now, curling wisps moving in a non-existent wind.

As though the God was not fully present in the city.

But the weight of Enki's presence, of a pure

disappointment, bore down on everyone – from Lucas who was close to the top of the tower, to those bunched down at the base, where the water had reached their knees.

The God raised an elongated arm, fingers so long as to be insect-like, and pointed at the mob. *Answer for your failures as a city.*

But no-one could speak. Not Lucas, Kiri or Fox, none of them.

"Why are you punishing them?" Reed called.

Gasps followed his question.

The Radiant King turned to Reed. *How kind of you to worry, Reed Lavender.*

Chapter 22.

"Do you?" Reed replied, but he found himself taking a step back. He set the boy down, but braced himself before the lad, grinding his teeth against the force of the God. It filled the air like a faint burning, insistent and heavy, but didn't seem to be an indicator of the true, as yet unreturned strength of the God.

Only if I didn't care would I absolve them without cause.

Reed glanced beyond the mob to the city streets but they were empty – no-one nearby to help, and the water was continuing to rise.

He lifted Potter's scythe, knuckles whitening as he looked up to Enki. Ridiculous to go up against a returning God, even with the true Scythe of a Reaper. *But what else do I have? I have to try something to weaken him. Is Ninhursag even here?* "So, you're giving up, then?"

And what do you mean by that, human?

"One failure and you're ready to throw the whole experiment away?"

Enki flung a distended arm out – tearing through the top

of the water tower within a blink, leaving Lucas clinging to the rungs a bare few feet below. Hunks of stone arced forth, flying clear of the people but landing with cracking splashes. *Without Feronia or your most-useful parents, it is rebirth or death in this very moment.*

"Not strong enough yourself?" Reed called.

The blackened rays loomed over him, moving so fast that he did not even have time to raise his weapon higher. The same blazing eyes bored down into him, a human-like face that stretched down into what might have been a mouth... but without a lower jaw.

Perhaps, perhaps not. But I have you to be sure.

Enki's hand brushed the scythe aside and a pair of fingers encircled his torso. The Radiant King lifted, moving so fast that the world blurred.

Ice erupted.

Reed screamed – even with the protection of Potter's robe, the slicing cold that spread from his torso was overwhelming.

You understand now, Reed Lavender. The pain faded, as though the God gave him enough respite to speak. *Do join me willingly, for I would not waste more of you in a pointless struggle.*

"No."

I seek no more disappointments.

Reed frowned. *He's coercing me, why?* Talk of disappointment and explanations? Was Enki weak enough after all? *I haven't come close to landing any sort of blow. At all. He has all the cards here.* The only thing close would have been... the mob! "Aren't you the disappointment, Enki?"

What claim is this?

"It's clear that *you* failed *them*."

I did not force any to choose chaos. To turn on one another.

"You wouldn't need to blame your children if you had taught them properly!"

Shadow grew from the soot-stained rays and this time the Radiant King's voice rose in volume. *I disagree.* And despite the ice that sliced into Reed again, it was clear that the God's words were a denial, tinged with doubt.

White flashed.

A giant serpent appeared behind the Radiant King, rising in a blazing outline of pale fire, dancing close.

It snapped forward to strike, bright fangs biting deep.

Enki spun with a roar. His free hand snapped around the scales but the serpent did not let go. Reed hissed as his own vision dimmed, Enki draining his strength. At the same time, colour spread through the serpent's head, a royal blue tinged with purple.

Ninhursag?

The Radiant King continued to struggle and his voice grew storm-like – but in a muted, distant manner, as though all the fury were contained. His desperation bled through too, a taint in the air something bitter Reed could taste, forcing a gag.

But colour continued to spread through the serpent, rapidly as Enki weakened further; his grip on Reed began to falter, fingers peeling free.

Reed struggled and with the God's shaken grip came relief from the draining that threatened Reed himself.

The hand opened.

Air rushed over him as he fell, flailing to right himself – only to smack into the water. Bubbles surged and then he hit the earth too, hard but not hard enough to break any bones. *The bruises are going to be dark though.*

But he was free!

He found his feet and burst free in a surge of relief, finding himself in chest-deep water. Above, Ninhursag continued to drag the now-fading Enki down. Her fangs seemed to be drawing in everything about the God, her former consort unable to fight back.

Wails of despair came from the mob, but Reed churned water as he spun, searching for the boy…

There!

The kid was treading water, lying on his back, drifting slowly away from the tower.

"Are you all right?" Reed called as he sloshed near.

Not too bad, I think.

"Good." Reed kept a hold of the boy as he stared at the Radiant King sinking further down, shrinking, a total lessening of colour and presence. *Ninhursag* had absorbed him. *And it didn't seem too hard for her. Did I really provide a final chink in his armour? Reveal the supposed bitter truth?*

The serpent rose, forked tongue flicking between fangs, scales swirling with blues, reds and yellows – but each colour deep, as though pushing through a layer of black clouds. Beautiful enough… but what did it mean? *Is Enki part of Ninhursag now?*

She's leaving.

The boy was right. Ninhursag was turning translucent, the tops of buildings and clouds visible through her body and then the sky was empty, leaving a silence in her place. A chill snuck under Reed's skin.

Did we just create some sort of super-goddess?

Chapter 23.

In time, the water had receded, leaving earth and asphalt unsettled, dotted with warm, sunset-puddles and tiny, shallow lakes.

Kiri had led the people of Parginos – those who had not already fled into the city – in a tired and downcast group away from the tower and toward Raelene's shop where she planned to feed them. The shop probably wouldn't fit everyone comfortably, but maybe the food and togetherness would offer distraction and comfort...

Max was right. The people of Enki's practice city would need a new home; they'd need someone to help them, especially if the blank stares and shuffling gait were indicators. Although among all of them, the telepathic boy whose name Reed had not learnt, seemed to be handling things the best.

Emma took his arm. "Max and Lina are ready if you are."

"I guess so," he replied, glancing at her. She was smiling, her hair graced with gold from the sunset that poured in between buildings. "So, you didn't tell me, what did you think of Kiri's maze?"

"Pure nightmare-fuel."

"Sounds about right," he said with a grin.

Nearby, Max, Lina and the others had gathered, speaking together softly. This time, the 'others' didn't just include Diego, Adrina and the wolves, but Patrick too. He stood in his gym polo, laughing along with Devin but every now and then he glanced around, as if expecting to be thrust back into... wherever Enki had stored him.

It didn't make much sense to Reed, much like the location of Parginos itself, but it had apparently taken Adrina and Diego a significant amount of time to rescue him.

And while at least some of the preparations everyone had taken before returning to Parginos had been of use, in the end it wasn't the song or bells but Ninhursag that saved them.

"Did Max or Lina have anything to say about Ninhursag?" he asked.

"Not really. They're hiding it but they seem pretty tired themselves – if that's something that can happen to the children of Death."

He nodded. "We probably owe those two just as much as Ninhursag."

"Yeah. And Max probably won't stop boasting about it, either," Emma said. "Although, he *is* disappointed that their staff broke." As a channel for the Sumerian Goddess, it had worked beautifully, but at the cost of whatever remained of Feronia, *and* the wand itself. *It must have been an important item for Max to be upset; wonder who he borrowed it from?*

Reed sighed.

"What's wrong? Shouldn't we be celebrating at least a little?"

"We should but I don't know if I can leave just yet..."

"Oh." Emma gave his arm a squeeze. "Sorry, I can't believe I forgot. Have you seen her since?"

"No. I'm looking but I just can't sense anything."

"Maybe you need to ask your aunty?"

He gestured to the robe. "Like this?"

"Whatever gets you out of that thing soonest," Emma said. "You still look like him now and then, even when I know what's going on."

"I guess I'd need to bring Potter with me." *Maybe she'll be willing to listen, now that we've succeeded. Even overlook my escape?*

Max appeared before him. "Excellent idea. How about I let Lina keep an eye on things here, then we get Adrina and Diego to send everyone home, including the lovely Emma here. Then, you and I can find Potter and go and update Mother together."

"Think she'll accept what we've done?"

"Yes."

Reed chuckled. "Wow, no hesitation there, cousin."

"Precisely, especially since you found Mother's own sister; she'll be thrilled."

The word 'thrilled' has never come to mind when I think of Aunty. "Maybe."

"Do you have much choice?" Emma asked. "You literally cannot hide from Death, Reed. You have to take the chance."

She's right. He leant in and kissed her. "Back soon."

Chapter 24.

"This is her garden, isn't it?" Reed asked. He stood with Max and Potter – the Reaper now clothed as himself – in a quiet place of stone. Black, grey, white and powder blue, the rock garden contained no plant life but instead, a single square bench seat in the open centre.

Before the bench, in a large display case of glass that floated a few feet above the ground, rested a flintlock pistol. The weapon was of polished wood, the curved butt and trigger guard giving it an elegant look. The only other time Reed had visited Aunty's garden was as a child and back then, there had been a dagger inside.

"It changes every visit," Max said. "She seems very curious about humans and weapons."

"Why?"

"The rush to death that such items represent," Potter said, his usual passive tone not tinted with impatience this time.

Aunt Mors appeared upon the bench.

Children. You have exceeded my expectations and at the same time, I wonder.

"You seem quite reflective, Mother," Potter said.

Perhaps.

"Then you'll forgive Reed and let him stay?" Max asked. "I'm sure you know he was pivotal."

I do, Maximilian – as was our original hope. And I suppose I might even overlook Potter's indiscretions too.

"Thank you."

Reed controlled a frown with some difficulty. *She's being awfully reasonable, and that's somehow a little troubling.* "Then can we search for my mother again?"

I sense her now; she is seeking more of herself. I will be watching and I trust you will be able to speak with her again. No doubt she will seek you out soon.

Reed nodded. *Okay, that's actually comforting to hear... maybe Aunty cares more than I assumed?*

"What about Ninhursag?" Potter asked. "Does she hide still?"

Verily. And we will watch for her as well, without malice but studiously, for it is a curious thing and one that does not happen often.

"Then everything worked out pretty well for everyone, didn't it?" Max said with a big grin.

Aunty Mors stood. *There is one for whom I cannot say that is precisely true. Katarina has uncovered something. She will seek your assistance with the matter, Reed.*

"Katarina? She's the one like me, isn't she?"

Yes.

"What's happened?"

It is a Rogue. I will let her explain but in order to help her, you will have to deal with that police matter first.

Reed blinked.

And not at her comment about the police, true as it was – but it was the word 'Rogue' that rang in his ears.

A Reaper who had abandoned all ties with the family. A Reaper using their powers for ill purposes, to kill and worse. But they did not operate in a manner that would simply have them Vanished or punished by the Gods.

Rogues were hardly so foolish, for they hid behind human surrogates in order to prey upon humans, forcing the gods to send Surrogates, as per the sacrosanct rules.

Rules that too often allowed for so much suffering.

Rules that people like me were made for.

"Where is she now?" Reed asked.

Travelling from the seaside. You have three days, Reed. Prepare your human methods but do not overlook your family.

"Then I have permission to use Max, Lina and the others?"

Express permission.

Reed glanced at Max and Potter, their expressions muted, then back to Aunty. "Is something different about this Rogue?"

Yes. It is a Lamia.

"*Lamia*? That's Latin for vampire, isn't it? Vampires don't exist here. And do you mean that she's part Vampire, part Reaper?"

She is from afar. And yes.

Reed gaped.

I trust you have more to offer than shock, Reed.

He spread his hands. "But, the wards and warnings. Why weren't they tripped when she entered?"

That is a question to which Katarina has not discovered satisfactory answers yet – save your own questions for her. But, while you wait for her, deal with your police matters and seek out a True Priest.

"I will," he said. *The best way deal with a fallen angel, I guess.*

Max placed a hand on his shoulder. "Do you think whoever we work with will like jokes about clergymen and bars?"

A Note from Ashley

Hello! I hope you enjoyed *Summer in the City* and thanks for reading.

I'd like to ask if you could help me out by leaving an honest review of the book at your place of purchase? Long or short, bad or good, it all helps!

AND if you'd like to sign up to my newsletter (at www.ashleycapes.com) you'll be the first to know when the fourth Reed Lavender story is released. You'll also have first access to preview chapters and pre-release editions of the story, in addition to being automatically added into the draw for giveaways.

Ashley

ACKNOWLEDGMENTS

It's been a little while now but I'm still enjoying writing stories about Reed and his cousins and so I most definitely plan to write more, especially since I've heard from folks telling me they've enjoyed the books.

And of course, as always, I want to thank Brooke for her constant support and belief in my work, and also for once again lending her awesome editing skills!

Also, to everyone who works hard to help me at every stage of the process, but especially once more to Rebekah at VividCovers for yet another great cover.

You might also enjoy other books from Ashley:

A Whisper of Leaves

When young teacher Riko finds an old journal buried in the forests beneath Mt Fuji, a malevolent, untraceable force begins to threaten her at every turn.

But is it all in her head?

The more she studies the journal for answers, the more questions she uncovers. Worse, no-one takes her fears seriously and her best lead appears to be a belligerent old man, whose only care in the world is raking leaves deep in the forest.

With her grip on reality shaken and friendships strained to breaking point, Riko must discover the truth about the journal in order to put ghosts of the past to rest before she loses everything.

A mysterious ghost-story full of suspense!

You might also enjoy other books from Ashley:

Crossings

Deep in the Australian forests, something dark is stirring.

When wildlife ranger Lisa Thomas finds a pile of animal entrails on her doorstep she immediately suspects her abusive ex, but the sudden spate of deaths that follow seem beyond even Ben's vindictiveness.

Worse, her father's health is deteriorating fast and when the harassment and deaths continue, it only fuels her feelings of powerlessness. To add confusion to growing fear, Lisa must also investigate reports of a giant white kangaroo, reports that suggest the creature is no mere hoax.

Yet the mysterious kangaroo is impossible to track down and the more Lisa searches the more she's sure an even greater threat lurks in the wilderness...